GORDON KORMAN
BRUNO & BOOTS
BEWARE THE FISH!

ISBN 0-590-41802-5

12 11 10 9 8 7 6 5 4 3   8 9/8 0 1 2/9

For Patrick J. Rankin, genius

Contents

Beware The Fish!

THE FISH:

William R. Sturgeon, Headmaster of Macdonald Hall, a kind, understanding, yet firm administrator who is secretly very fond of his students.

THE FISH:

An unknown terrorist leader who is using public communications to send messages to members of his evil organization.

THE FISH:

A large labelled diagram of the Pacific salmon that hangs on the wall in the room of eccentric genius Elmer Drimsdale.

Much ado about spinach

Few people would argue that Macdonald Hall, located east of Toronto just off Highway 48, is not the best boarding school for boys in Canada. Even the most severe critics of modern education point to the ivy-covered walls of the Hall as a symbol of the happy blend of tradition, enlightened administration and progressive educational policies that have resulted in a rare combination of pleased parents and contented students.

Why, then, are rumblings echoing from the dining hall?

* * *

"Yes! Okay! So we need another vegetable! But why spinach?" exclaimed Boots O'Neal in disgust.

"Stewed green leaves," agreed Bruno Walton, pushing the spinach as far from the rest of his dinner as he could without actually toppling it off his plate onto the tray. "Last week they started serving raisins and figs instead of cake and ice cream. Now it's spinach instead of french fries. If this keeps up I'll be the healthiest person ever to starve to death at this school. Yeccch!"

The other boys at the dining hall table murmured their agreement.

"I told you before," said Larry Wilson, the Headmaster's office messenger, "it's the dietician. I heard Mr. Sturgeon tell her to cut costs but keep the nutrition the same."

"They're trying to kill us all!" moaned big Wilbur Hackenschleimer, who was used to having triple helpings of everything.

"You cannot possibly die," put in studious Elmer Drimsdale, "on this diet. It is nutritionally and chemically balanced." He methodically deposited some spinach into his mouth.

"You can die if you don't eat it," retorted Bruno. "We're starving! This isn't *food*!"

"Seems to me Macdonald Hall is doing a lot of cost-cutting lately," complained Boots. "Yesterday someone kicked the soccer ball out onto the highway and it got run over by a truck. End of ball, end of game. Can you imagine a school this size owning only one soccer ball?"

"And they've stopped our evening snack," added Wilbur miserably.

"I never considered it," said Elmer thoughtfully, "but the science laboratory is very low on materials and they're not being replenished. The big microscope has

2

been broken for a week, but Mr. Hubert has made no move to have it repaired."

"No cereal at bedtime," mourned Wilbur.

"The office is crazy for saving paper," added Larry. "And Mr. Sturgeon is using straight pins instead of paper clips and staples."

"At least The Fish gets to eat food," said Wilbur sadly. "I'll bet Mrs. Sturgeon doesn't cook garbage like this for him."

"And the thermostats are nailed at twenty in the dormitories," Boots pointed out. "Bruno and I almost froze to death last night."

"The food used to be so good here," Wilbur reminisced.

Suddenly Bruno pounded his fist onto the table. The others jumped and turned their eyes towards him.

"Something's wrong," he declared. "The Hall was never like this before. The Fish always used to stand up for us and get us the things we needed. Why isn't he doing it now?"

Nobody answered.

"Larry," Bruno went on, a determined gleam in his eyes, "when you're on duty around the office, keep on the lookout. If we can find out why this is happening, we can do something about it."

"You've got it," agreed Larry. "I'll try."

* * *

"Mildred," Mr. Sturgeon, Headmaster of Macdonald Hall, announced to his wife, "I see no alternative. I am going to resign."

"Now, William," she said soothingly, "what good would that do?"

"The situation has become intolerable!" he exclaimed, pacing the small living room of the Headmaster's residence. "The budget is constantly being cut. My students are being deprived—not just of treats and luxuries, but of necessary school supplies as well. I cannot sit by and watch this going on, yet I can't do anything about it. My only course is resignation."

"That's the easy way out," his wife accused him. "You'd be abandoning our boys if you just quit. Why can't you stay on and fight?"

Mr. Sturgeon stopped pacing and eased himself into the rocking chair by the window. "I'd love to fight," he replied, "but I have nothing to fight with. The trustees do —enrolment is down and costs are soaring. They're not giving me enough money to run Macdonald Hall properly. The fact is, Mildred, if this keeps up we're going to lose the school."

"Oh, dear! Can it be that bad?"

He nodded emphatically. "At the last Board meeting there was some serious talk of putting the land and buildings up for sale."

"But this has been our home for eighteen years!"

The Headmaster shrugged unhappily. "What can I

4

do?" He sighed. "But you do have a point. The captain should go down with the ship. I'll stay on."

* * *

Friday evening, just before midnight, the silence of the moonlit campus was disturbed by the squeaking of the window of room 306 in Dormitory 3. Bruno Walton and Boots O'Neal scrambled over the sill and jumped to the ground. They darted across the tree-lined campus, crossed the highway and nimbly scaled the wrought-iron fence around Miss Scrimmage's Finishing School for Young Ladies.

"It's a good thing we've got this place handy," said Bruno in an undertone. "If Cathy and Diane weren't feeding us we'd starve to death!" He picked up a handful of pebbles and tossed them at a second-storey window.

Cathy Burton's dark head appeared over the sill. "Your provisions will be right down," she called softly.

A few moments later a large paper bag came sailing out the window and landed at their feet. Printed on the bag in green was the message: *Happy eating. Courtesy of Miss Scrimmage's Finishing School for Young Ladies, Cathy Burton and Diane Grant, Caterers.*

Boots looked up at the open window. "You've just saved a couple of lives," he called.

"Our pleasure," answered Cathy. "Any time. Just don't expect trading stamps." She waved, then shut the window.

The boys grabbed the food parcel and retraced their steps to the Macdonald Hall campus and their own Dormitory 3. They climbed back into their room.

Boots shut the window as, still in the dark, Bruno hurled himself onto his bed. There was a wild, terrified scream. Squinting in the moonlight, Boots could just make out the figure of his roommate struggling on the floor with an unknown assailant. Without hesitation he threw himself into the battle. Arms and legs thrashed. Muffled grunts filled the room. Boots could feel the intruder slowly forcing him into a headlock. He reached out blindly, grabbed a foot and started twisting.

There was a sudden click and the light came on. The arm around Boots's neck was Bruno's; the hand twisting Bruno's foot was Boots's. Standing by the light switch, pale and shaking, was Larry Wilson.

"Douse that light!" Bruno gasped angrily. "Do you want The Fish on our necks?"

Larry switched off the overhead light. "Sorry," he said, still stunned.

"What the heck are you doing in our room?" demanded Boots as he and Bruno disentangled themselves and stood up.

"You asked me to keep my ears open," Larry complained. "I came here to report, not to get beaten up. You guys were out, so I lay down to wait for you. I guess I fell asleep. Do you think the racket woke up the Housemaster?"

Boots laughed. "Wake up Mr. Fudge? Don't you know about him?"

"Old Fudgie wouldn't wake up if an express train passed under his bed," said Bruno. "The first year we were here at the Hall, Boots and I came back from Scrimmage's one night and climbed into his room by mistake. If that kind of laughing in his ear won't wake him up, nothing will."

"You said you heard something," Boots reminded their visitor. "What's up?"

"You aren't going to like this very much," Larry said nervously.

"Oh, no," groaned Bruno. "I suppose they've eliminated lunch."

"Worse than that," said Larry. "The Fish has given orders to close up Dormitory 3."

There was a long moment of stunned silence.

Bruno was the first to find his voice. "No," he said quietly. "They can't do that. This is our home."

"It's being done," said Larry. "Tomorrow the orders will go out telling you where to move."

"We won't go!" stormed Boots. "We'll barricade ourselves in and hold out to the end!"

"Why?" cried Bruno. "Why would The Fish do this to us? Why?"

"Well," said Larry, "no one has actually said it, but it looks to me as if Macdonald Hall is going broke. They can't afford to run three dorms any more."

"Then let them close 1! Or 2!" howled Bruno. "But not ours! It's not fair!"

"What if you get sent to one room and me to another?" put in Boots in a strangled voice.

"No, no," soothed Larry. "You two guys are both being sent to 201."

There was another shocked silence.

"Elmer Drimsdale!" Bruno and Boots howled in unison.

"I can't live with Elmer Drimsdale!" cried Boots. "He's crazy!"

"Oh, no!" moaned Bruno, who had once been Elmer's roommate. "No, no, *no*!"

"But you guys are friends of Elmer's," Larry said, mystified.

"Yes, but that's a lot different from *living* with him!" Bruno exclaimed. "Elmer keeps ants! And fish in the bathtub! And plants all over the place! And he's always performing some experiment that takes up half the room! And he gets up at six in the morning!"

"What have we done to deserve this?" asked Boots in despair.

Bruno felt around in the dark, located the bag from Cathy and Diane and ripped it open. "Let's eat," he suggested glumly. "I always suffer better on a full stomach."

The three boys began to eat the assortment of cookies, fruit and cheese filched for them by Miss Scrimmage's girls.

"I'm getting sent to Dormitory 2 as well," Larry told them as he savoured the almost forgotten taste of a chocolate chip cookie. "I'll be across the hall in 204."

"204!" Bruno laughed despite his unhappiness. "That's Sidney Rampulsky. Be sure you pay up your accident insurance. That guy could trip over a moonbeam."

"At least he doesn't keep ants," moaned Boots.

"You know," said Bruno thoughtfully, "we're losing sight of the most important thing in this whole mess. If Macdonald Hall really is going broke, then we won't only be out of a dormitory. We'll be out of a school!"

"We're going broke, all right," said Larry. "Today I took a phone call from a real-estate company. Maybe the Hall is being put up for sale."

In the darkness of room 306, Bruno Walton's face took on a look of grim determination. "That does it!" he exclaimed. "They're starving us, they're forcing us out of our dorm, and now they're selling our school right out from under us! We won't let this happen!"

Boots, who had long ago learned to recognize the beginning of one of Bruno's crusades, felt a twinge of uneasiness. "This is all management and high finance," he protested. "It's even above The Fish. What can *we* do about it?"

"Well, I know what we *can't* do," replied Bruno. "We can't just sit back and let the Hall go down the drain! And that's exactly why the Macdonald Hall Preservation Society is meeting tomorrow at lunch!"

I never get caught

The following Saturday morning Miss Scrimmage's girls were enjoying a delightful brunch on the front lawn of the school. At the head of the table Miss Scrimmage herself was pouring tea. Unnoticed by her, two girls had stolen away to the apple orchard adjoining the school. From halfway up a large tree Cathy Burton was staring across the road through her binoculars.

"I told you something weird was going on at the Hall," she called down to her blonde roommate, Diane Grant. "The whole place is in an uproar. It looks as if they're moving or something."

"Moving where?" asked Diane, mystified.

"That's just it," was the reply. "They're not moving anywhere. They just seem to be walking around with suitcases and beds. And bumping into each other a lot."

"Can you see Bruno or Boots?" Diane asked.

"There they are," said Cathy. "Boots is just standing there. And Bruno's sitting on the biggest pile of stuff you

10

ever saw!"

"Catherine! Diane!" Miss Scrimmage came marching into the orchard, her expression severe. "Young ladies do not perch about in trees, nor do they leave the table without permission. You will be restricted to your room this evening and every evening this week. Return to your places at once."

"Don't worry," whispered Cathy to Diane as she dropped to the ground. "They'll let us in on it soon enough."

* * *

Across the road, the objects of their attention were busy hauling beds and belongings from Dormitory 3 to the other two buildings. In the midst of the hubbub, Bruno Walton had flopped down on his possessions. "You go on without me," he said dramatically to Boots. "I'll be along—eventually."

"Come on," said Boots. "Let's get there and get it over with!" They were both finding it hard to leave 306.

Reluctantly Bruno struggled to his feet. The two boys piled their belongings on top of the bed and began to carry the whole arrangement towards Dormitory 2.

"It's a good thing," Bruno muttered, "that Elmer has a spare bed. It would kill me if we had to carry two of them!"

They managed to struggle into the building and down the hall to room 201. Bruno kicked the door open.

"Hi, Elmer. It's us. We're moving in."

Elmer turned from his desk where he had been peering through a microscope and making notes.

"Hello," he greeted them. "Come right in. You can put the bed right over—uh—where *can* you put the bed?"

The room was already filled almost to capacity. A large fish tank gurgled on top of the bureau, and a huge sand-filled terrarium—the home of Elmer's ant colony—perched beside it. Books were piled everywhere, and an assortment of peculiar-looking devices lined the walls. On every available surface a plant pot stood. There was a fern, a trailing ivy, a Venus fly-trap, a desert yucca and, pride of the collection, a two-metre cactus currently in flower. There were also countless unidentifiable herbs and fungi. The only wall decoration was a large labelled diagram of the Pacific salmon. It was rumoured at Macdonald Hall that Elmer kept an endless supply of these in case the one in use became shabby.

Bruno indicated a complicated-looking mechanical device standing against the wall. "Why don't we move that electro-formionic impulse pussy-footer, or whatever it is?" he suggested.

"Oh, we can't do that," said Elmer. "It's bolted to the floor. You'll just have to put the bed in front of the door."

"But how will we get in and out?" asked Boots, more concerned with getting out than in.

"We'll have to climb over it," said Elmer. He peered at

Boots earnestly through his large horn-rimmed glasses. "You don't mind, do you?"

"Oh, no, of course not," said Boots, thinking longingly of nice, roomy 306. He cast a stricken glance at Bruno.

Bruno shrugged.

*　*　*

"Listen!" cried Sidney "Butterfingers" Rampulsky indignantly across the lunch table. "Everyone drops a clock now and then!"

"But you dropped *my* clock!" protested Larry Wilson, his new roommate. "And you broke it!"

"Well, I cut my finger on the glass," protested Sidney. "Don't I get any sympathy for that?" He held up a bandaged finger to support his claim.

"No," said Larry sourly. "If Macdonald Hall didn't have to keep a klutz like you in bandages it wouldn't be in such a pickle now."

"That pickle," Bruno Walton cut in, "is what we're here to discuss."

"They cut out pickles five weeks ago," sighed Wilbur Hackenschleimer.

"I thought we were here to eat." Boots looked with distaste at a dainty cucumber sandwich. "But I guess I was wrong about that."

Ignoring them, Bruno got up and surveyed the table. Larry and Sidney were still glaring at each other. Big Wilbur Hackenschleimer sat dreaming of a triple-decker hamburger with the works. Pete Anderson, who was now rooming with Wilbur, Elmer Drimsdale, Boots and himself made up the rest of the committee.

"Macdonald Hall is in trouble," Bruno announced dramatically, "and the responsibility of saving it rests with *us*, the Macdonald Hall Preservation Society!"

The boys looked at him uneasily—Bruno's causes were notorious.

"I'm having enough trouble saving myself," said Wilbur. "Besides the fact that they're not feeding us, what's wrong with Macdonald Hall?"

"I'll tell you what's wrong," exclaimed Bruno. "It's going down the tube! They may even put it up for sale!"

"That's ridiculous," snapped Pete. "The Fish would never allow it!"

"The Fish is only Headmaster," Bruno reminded him. "He doesn't own the place; he just works here. He's a victim, like the rest of us."

"I don't believe it," said Sidney flatly.

"Believe it," said Larry. "I'm The Fish's messenger. I'm around to hear what goes on in his office, and it's true."

"What do you think all these economy measures are for?" added Boots.

"That's right," agreed Bruno. "It's a bad situation and we've—"

The salt shaker in Elmer's hand slipped from his fingers and clattered to the table. He raised astounded, owl-like eyes to Bruno. "Do you mean that Macdonald Hall is going bankrupt?"

"We just finished saying that, Elmer," said Bruno patiently. Although Elmer was the school's genius, he was not known for his quick grasp of everyday matters. "Pay attention. This is very important if we're going to save the school."

"But what can *we* do?" asked Pete. "We're just students."

"Well, it seems to me," said Bruno who had, as usual, taken over the proceedings, "that if we can do something really great and get a lot of coverage in the newspapers and on radio and TV, then we'll get all sorts of new students. Everybody'll want to send their boys to a school where such terrific things happen."

"Sounds good to me," said Sidney.

"What terrific things?" asked Boots cautiously. He had been involved too many times before in Bruno's outrageous schemes.

"Well, that's going to be the hard part," admitted Bruno. "I haven't thought of any yet. But I'll have a suggestion box outside our room—that's 201—right after lunch. Talk it up a lot so all the guys will know. I want that box full of suggestions by morning. If we don't come up with an idea to put this place on the map, then we don't deserve to keep Macdonald Hall!"

* * *

After lunch Bruno, Boots and Elmer went back to Dormitory 2 and climbed over Boots's bed into their room.

"Elmer, what have you got for a suggestion box?" asked Bruno. "Ah—there's something." He reached down and tapped a large black box that sat on the floor by the bureau.

"No!" cried Elmer. "Don't touch that! It's extremely delicate electronic equipment. I'm working on a new theory of video broadcasting."

"Hot gazoobies!" said Bruno happily. "Our first suggestion. You invent some new TV thing and we'll get all sorts of publicity. But I still haven't got a suggestion box. I know, we'll use Boots's suitcase." He picked up a canvas duffle bag, zipped it open, dumped the contents on the floor and smiled in triumph. "Come on, Boots. Make yourself useful. Draw up a sign saying *Suggestion Box*."

"Can I pick my clothes up off the floor first, *sir*?" asked Boots sarcastically.

"Oh, we'll help you do that," Bruno replied cheerfully. "Elmer, pick up his clothes. Hurry up with that sign, Boots. I'm expecting millions of suggestions."

"And what will you be doing, oh master?"

Bruno hurled himself onto his new bed and wriggled until he was quite comfortable. "I thought I'd take a nap," he replied. "We've got to get to Scrimmage's tonight."

"Why?" asked Boots. "We've got plenty of food left."

"We need the girls' suggestions," said Bruno. "And," he added, "it wouldn't hurt to get in a little more food. Don't forget, we're begging for three now."

Elmer was touched.

* * *

Elmer was not quite so touched at midnight when he found that he was expected to accompany the expedition to Scrimmage's.

"But—but it's against the rules! If we get caught we'll be punished!"

"Agreed," said Bruno. "But I never get caught, so punishment is out of the question. Come on, Elm, live dangerously for once in your life!"

"Come on, Elmer," grinned Boots. "Those are *girls* over there."

"That's just it," said Elmer. "Girls make me extremely nervous. I simply cannot talk to them. My tongue dries up and my throat closes."

"Well, this is a good time to start learning," decided Bruno. "Come on, Elmer, it's for your own good." He nodded at Boots, and between the two of them they hustled Elmer out the window and dragged him across the campus and the highway. Before he knew it he was climbing the wrought-iron fence and then watching Bruno toss pebbles at the second-storey window.

When Cathy and Diane stuck their heads out, Elmer ducked behind Boots.

"*More* food?" Cathy called in disbelief.

"That too," said Bruno. "But we have to talk to you. We're coming up."

One by one, with much hoarse protesting from Elmer, the three boys shinnied up the drainpipe and were helped in through the window by Cathy and Diane.

Cathy regarded the skinny, crew-cut boy who stood cowering before them. "I see we have a newcomer," she observed.

"You know Elmer Drimsdale," said Bruno.

"By reputation." She grinned. "We haven't been introduced. Hi, I'm Cathy."

Elmer made a strangled noise deep in his throat.

"And I'm Diane," said the blonde girl. When there was no reply she glanced questioningly at Bruno. "Doesn't he talk?"

"No, I do not," croaked Elmer.

"He's a little nervous," explained Boots. "It's something to do with his tongue and his throat. We live with Elmer now. The Hall closed down Dormitory 3 and kicked us out of our room."

"That's terrible!" exclaimed Cathy. "Uh—I mean—no offence, Elmer."

"That's what all the ruckus was about then," said Diane. "All that running around with beds and everything."

Boots nodded gravely.

"Now down to business," said Bruno. "We're in big trouble."

"So what else is new?" asked Cathy with a grin.

"No, he doesn't mean us; he means Macdonald Hall," said Boots. "The Hall is going bankrupt. We could close up soon. You girls could end up with a slaughterhouse across the road instead of us."

"*What*?" shrieked Cathy.

"No, no," soothed Elmer, finally regaining his voice. "The zoning bylaws would never permit a slaughterhouse. A large sewage-treatment plant, perhaps. I understand the city is looking for a place to locate one."

"*Oh, no!*" cried Diane, appalled.

"Well," Elmer added dubiously, "perhaps it will only be a highrise apartment complex."

Cathy and Diane moaned in unison.

"Wait a minute, wait a minute," Bruno put in. "You're not getting any of that stuff across the road because we are going to save Macdonald Hall. We're going to get so much great publicity that enrolment will double and there won't be any reason to close the school."

"What's our job?" asked Cathy.

"We'll do anything!" Diane put in.

"We need publicity," said Bruno. "Your job right now is to figure out how we're going to get it."

"Tell all the girls," Boots added. "We need all the suggestions we can get."

"We'll be back in a couple of days," said Bruno, "to hear what you've come up with." Behind him, Elmer groaned. This adventure, he was certain, was enough to fill his lifetime quota of excitement. Having Bruno and Boots as roommates was not going to be easy.

"Now," said Bruno, "how about some food?"

Diane tiptoed to the door. "Be right back," she whispered.

True to her word, she was back in less than five minutes, carrying the usual paper bag. "Sandwiches tonight," she told them. "Part of tomorrow's lunch."

"We'd better get going," Boots suggested anxiously.

Bruno took the bag and stuffed it into Boots's hand. He swung a leg over the window ledge. "Thanks for the grub. Work hard on those suggestions." He started to shinny down. Boots followed, and Elmer, anxious not to be left alone with the girls, was right behind him.

Bruno's feet hit the ground with a thud.

"Halt!" cried a voice.

Just as Boots slipped to the ground behind Bruno, a beam of light illuminated the two of them.

At the top of the drainpipe, Elmer, frozen with fear, felt hands grasp at his arms. Cathy and Diane hauled him back up over the sill and into the room.

"Stay down!" Cathy whispered. "It's Miss Scrimmage! She's got Bruno and Boots!"

"I thought I heard screams!" said Miss Scrimmage, pointing a shotgun at the two boys. "You should be ashamed of yourselves, coming over here and terrorizing my poor innocent girls! Hands over your heads!" Her hair curlers bounced as she gestured with the shotgun towards the highway. "Now quick-march back to Macdonald Hall! I'm taking you to Mr. Sturgeon! Move, both of you!"

Bruno looked around. There *were* only two of them. What had happened to Elmer?

Miss Scrimmage, seething with indignation, marched them across the road and the Macdonald Hall campus to the Headmaster's cottage, which stood at the edge of the south lawn. Heedless of the fact that it was one o'clock in the morning and that she was in her dressing gown, she rang the bell insistently.

A few moments passed before Mr. Sturgeon appeared at the door in his red silk bathrobe and his bedroom slippers. He took in the scene with one horrified glance.

"Miss Scrimmage, put that weapon down this instant!" he exclaimed. "How dare you point it at any of my boys!"

"They are marauders!" Miss Scrimmage accused. "I caught them on our grounds terrorizing my poor, defenceless girls! You may consider yourself lucky that I did not simply turn them over to the police!"

The Headmaster hustled Bruno and Boots into his house and placed himself between them and Miss Scrimmage. "The police," he said in icy rage, "would be interested to know that you chase children around with guns in the dead of night. These boys will be dealt with. Good evening." He slammed the door in her face.

Mr. Sturgeon turned to Bruno and Boots to find his

wife comforting them.

"Mildred," he said, "please go back to bed."

She ignored him. "Bruno, Melvin, you poor boys! You must be awfully frightened! What were you doing over there?"

Wordlessly Boots held out the food parcel.

Mrs. Sturgeon opened the bag. "Sandwiches! Oh, William, they were hungry! I told you growing boys have to have their evening snack!"

"Enough of this!" exclaimed Mr. Sturgeon. He opened the door a crack and peered outside.

"Is the coast clear, sir?" asked Bruno in a small voice.

"You may go," barked Mr. Sturgeon, "but you will be in my office at eight tomorrow morning. Goodnight."

* * *

"Oh, Miss Scrimmage, it was just terrible!" quavered Cathy. "We were so scared! Thank goodness you saved us!"

Miss Scrimmage sat down on the bed under which Elmer Drimsdale cowered, paralyzed with fear. "You poor darlings," she said comfortingly. "You have nothing to fear while I am here. I can smell an intruder anywhere!"

Underneath the bed, some dust went up Elmer's nose. He sneezed.

"*Gezundheit*, dear," said Miss Scrimmage.

"Thank you," said Cathy and Diane both at the same

time.

"Would you two girls like me to spend the night in your room?" the Headmistress offered kindly.

"No!" cried Diane.

"What she means," said Cathy quickly, "is that she has this terrible cold—you heard her sneeze—and we wouldn't want you to catch it."

"Oh," said Miss Scrimmage. "How thoughtful of you. But Catherine might catch it too. Come along, Diane. To the infirmary with you. I shall look after you."

With a glance of pure hatred at her grinning room-mate, Diane followed Miss Scrimmage from the room.

Cathy dragged Elmer out from under the bed. "All clear," she said cheerfully.

Elmer mouthed the words, "I think I'm going to be sick." His voice was gone again.

"I can understand how this sort of thing might upset you, this being your first time here," she said sympatheti-cally. "I'll get a cold cloth for your head. You'll have to stick around for a couple of hours anyway, until the heat's off. Meanwhile, please make yourself comfortable. There's a nice bed over there. Diane won't be needing it tonight."

Elmer moaned and lay down, gingerly trying to sort out the events of the evening.

* * *

"Where can he be?" exclaimed Bruno for the umpteenth time, pacing the floor like a worried father.

"I don't care where he is!" cried Boots. "Bruno, will you think of *us* for a minute? The Fish is going to kill us tomorrow!"

"But what about Elmer? He's helpless! And we just left him there!" Bruno was stricken with guilt.

"We didn't leave him. We were marched away at gunpoint." Boots sighed miserably. "Don't worry, Bruno. The way our luck has been running tonight, he'll probably turn up safe and sound!"

Attention, world!

It was four o'clock in the morning when Bruno and Boots were awakened by a frantic scratching at the window. The two boys rushed over and pulled Elmer in.

He was a sight to behold. His face was shiny with perspiration, and his usually neat crew-cut was standing on end. He was twitching nervously and his eyes were wild. He looked like a hunted animal.

"Where have you been?" stormed Bruno. "We've been worried sick!"

His shaky knees collapsing under him, Elmer sat down on the floor to tell his tale of woe. "It was horrible!" he croaked. "After those two girls saved me from Miss Scrimmage they wouldn't let me leave! They made me hide under the bed! When Miss Scrimmage came in and sat down on the bed, I was terrified!"

Bruno and Boots could bear it no longer. They burst into uncontrollable laughter.

Elmer was outraged. "It's not amusing! And besides,

they told Miss Scrimmage the most horrid lies about you. They said you were terrorizing them until she came along and saved them!"

By this time Bruno and Boots had collapsed to the floor in hysterics.

"Then I had to stay there for three hours before that Cathy person would let me leave," Elmer continued. "It was the most harrowing experience of my life!"

"No more, Elmer!" gasped Bruno, exhausted. "I can't stand it!"

Boots caught his breath. "Not bad for a first time out! Elmer, I'm nominating you for Rookie of the Year!"

"It's all very well for you to laugh," protested Elmer reproachfully. "You didn't have to go through what I did."

"Hah!" said Boots. "Old Scrimmage marched us to The Fish at gunpoint and he almost had a fit! We've got to see him in the office at eight o'clock. We're cooked!"

Elmer turned even paler. "Does—does Mr. Sturgeon know about me?"

"No, he doesn't," said Boots. "You're clean."

Elmer sighed with relief and turned to Bruno. "You told me you never get caught," he accused. "Miss Scrimmage caught you."

Bruno shrugged. "It was a one-in-a-million chance," he said. "Even a pro like me can have an off night. There's no way it could ever happen again. She got lucky."

"Lucky or not," Boots said mournfully, "we're the ones who are going to have to face the music."

* * *

"William, what are you going to do to those poor boys?"

Mr. Sturgeon sipped his breakfast coffee. "I don't know, Mildred," he replied. "I am still Headmaster here, and roaming the countryside in the dead of night is frowned upon by this institution."

"But they were hungry," his wife pleaded. "They aren't getting enough to eat!"

"They *are* getting enough to eat," he snapped back. "They just aren't eating it." He shook his head. "I should be furious with them, but somehow I just feel angry at that awful Scrimmage woman. Every time I think of her being allowed to own that shotgun . . . If she ever hurts one of my boys, I'll—"

"William, you're shouting again."

* * *

At precisely 8 A.M., Bruno and Boots marched past the heavy oak door with *HEADMASTER* lettered in gold, and into the office. They ignored the comfortable chairs intended for visitors and automatically sat down on the hard wooden bench facing Mr. Sturgeon's desk.

The Headmaster leaned forward, fixing them with the cold, fish-like stare which made his nickname all the more appropriate.

"Lights-out at Macdonald Hall occurs at exactly ten

o'clock," he said icily. "From that moment on all students are expected to be in their beds. Miss Scrimmage's Finishing School for Young Ladies is off limits at all times, especially in the middle of the night. Are those rules something new to you?"

"No, sir," Bruno admitted quietly.

"I'm very happy to hear that," said Mr. Sturgeon. "I never want to catch you over there again. Is that understood?"

"Yes, sir," chorused Bruno and Boots.

"Excellent," said Mr. Sturgeon. "At least I'm glad to see you didn't involve Drimsdale in your nonsense. As for your punishment—except for mealtimes, you are to spend the rest of today in your room." He stood up. "Dismissed."

"Thank you, sir." The boys backed out of the office and scurried down the marble corridor of the Faculty Building.

Once outside, Boots let his breath out in a long sigh of relief. "A day's punishment?" he said incredulously. "I thought he was going to murder us!"

"I knew he'd go easy," replied Bruno. "He doesn't like Miss Scrimmage anyway. He was so mad at her he forgot he was mad at us. It's all very simple. Anyway, we need a quiet day in our room."

"You bet!" said Boots enthusiastically. "I could use a nap. I hardly slept at all last night."

"Who said anything about sleep?" demanded Bruno.

"Our suggestion box must be full by now. We have to get to work."

"Swell," said Boots without enthusiasm. "We could have started getting publicity for the Hall last night if we'd thought of it. Picture this: *Students Shot By Crazed Headmistress.* Wouldn't that have enlarged our enrolment?"

"Don't be an idiot," scoffed Bruno. "This is an important thing we're doing. If everyone takes it as lightly as you do and Macdonald Hall closes, then where will we be?"

The two boys headed for Dormitory 2 to serve their punishment and read the suggestions.

* * *

"I don't *care* about the budget!" snapped Mr. Sturgeon into the telephone. "My boys *must* have their evening snack ... Because they're young and healthy and they're growing, that's why. They're also begging food over at Scrimmage's, and I'll not have that! We may be in financial difficulty, but surely we have some pride! ... Yes, a little cereal and milk would be fine. I'm glad you agree, Jim ... Thank you. Goodbye."

He replaced the receiver with a look of satisfaction on his face. It had taken Bruno Walton and Melvin O'Neal to get him back into harness, but at least now he was fighting back.

* * *

In room 201 the Pacific salmon smiled down on industrious activity. Elmer Drimsdale's head was buried deep inside the black box containing his video invention. He was tinkering happily while humming a Bach fugue.

Bruno and Boots sat cross-legged on the floor. Between them was Boots's duffle bag, filled to overflowing with small pieces of paper.

"Here's something," said Boots. "*Let them close the place up so we can all go home and get a square meal.* It's signed *Anonymous.*"

"You know, I'm a little disappointed in all this," said Bruno. "A lot of the guys don't seem to have understood what we wanted. Look at these suggestions—*rob a bank, get caught and get your name in the paper; commit a murder*, same notation. What's the matter with these idiots?"

Boots laughed. "Here's one from Sidney Rampulsky. It says, *Discover gold on the campus.*"

"Ha!" said Bruno. "I wish we could. Here's two more *rob a bank*, for goodness' sake!" He shuffled through several others. "Hey! Now here's something! Marvin Trimble says we should fake an ancient Indian burial ground. Then the government will declare the site a national monument and they'll never allow anything to be built here, so the school will stay."

"Bruno, are you crazy?" Boots exclaimed. "We can't do that. Where would we get ancient relics?"

"An arrow is an arrow," shrugged Bruno.

"Not when it's plastic and says *Made in Japan*!"

"So we'll make a few in shop," argued Bruno, "and we'll stomp on them a bit so they'll look old."

"They won't be ancient enough," insisted Boots. "Those archeologist guys have ways of finding out how old things like that are. They're not just going to take a quick look and say, 'Great heavens! Arrows!' and then put up a national monument. They're going to check to see if the stuff is real—which it won't be. And then we'll be in trouble again."

"I guess you're right," conceded Bruno. "What a stupid guy that Marvin Trimble is! Do you see anything else in this mess?"

Boots nodded. "Rob Adams says someone should make a great discovery, like a cure for a terrible disease. Just like that!"

"That's Elmer's department," laughed Bruno. "Hey, Elm, as soon as you're finished with that TV thing would you mind discovering a cure for some dread disease?"

Elmer's head emerged from the black box. "Oh," he said seriously, "as a matter of fact I'm working on a cure for the common cold right now."

"I thought you were working on that broadcasting thing," said Boots.

"I am," replied Elmer. "I am currently involved in seventeen different projects—or is it eighteen? I don't remember." His head disappeared again.

Boots cast Bruno a look of pure wonder. "Does he ever finish anything? Is he ever successful?"

Bruno shrugged. "I don't know."

"At last!" cried Elmer. "It's completed!" He leaped to his feet and gazed earnestly at Bruno and Boots. "Would you mind helping me set it up to test it?"

"Sure," said Bruno.

He and Boots picked themselves up off the floor and watched in amazement as Elmer began gathering equipment from every corner of the room, under the beds and in the closet. They spent the next hour fetching, carrying and holding electronic gear for the eccentric genius as he set up his new invention. When it was all done, several yards of wire and cable snaked across the walls and under the furniture to Elmer's black box. On top of the box sat an enormous jumble of circuits, tubes and resistors, and a condensor microphone, all attached to a camera turret that was a full yard long. The lens was pointed directly at Elmer's Pacific salmon poster. On the back of the black box was a small television screen and speaker.

Bruno and Boots were awed.

"Wow!" said Boots. "I didn't think a mere mortal could make such a thing!"

"Wow!" echoed Bruno. "Even if it doesn't work, Elm, it's a thing of beauty! Now what happens?"

"We try it out, of course," replied Elmer. "If my computations are correct, my salmon should appear on the screen and whatever we say will come out on the adjacent speaker."

He reached for the *On* switch.

* * *

"Isn't this movie exciting, William?" said Mrs. Sturgeon. "I don't know when I've enjoyed an afternoon of television more. How do you think it's all going to turn out?"

"We'll know soon enough, Mildred," Mr. Sturgeon replied, glancing at his wristwatch. "The picture ends in five minutes, so the climax must be coming up soon."

The couple watched the action intently.

Suddenly there was a buzz of static and the screen went momentarily blank. The Sunday Matinee was replaced by a fuzzy image of a large fish, dead centre on the screen. It wavered once, then stabilized. The audio crackled into what sounded like distant cheering, and a garbled voice cried, *Attention, world! We bring you the Fish!*

This was followed by what sounded like laughter.

"William, what in the world—?"

Her husband frowned. "A fish. This is very strange indeed."

"But what is it?" she insisted.

Both stared in perplexed fascination for some time until at last the image of the mysterious fish faded out. It was replaced by the Sunday Matinee just as the words *The End* appeared on the screen.

"William, our movie is over!"

Mr. Sturgeon stared at the television screen. "*Attention world*," he mused. "*We bring you the Fish.*"

* * *

"Hot gazoobies, Elmer, it works!" screamed Bruno ecstatically, jumping up and down in the little space there was left in the room.

"It's fantastic!" cried Boots.

"Yes," agreed Elmer, flushed with pleasure. "It would appear that I am on the right track."

"Hey, I know!" exclaimed Bruno. "We can use this thing to show up on people's TV sets and tell them how great Macdonald Hall is and how they should send all their sons here!"

"No, no," Elmer smiled indulgently. "There is a problem in the equations. It's a new theory in circuitry—a curious contradition, you might say. This is a preliminary experimental model. It will only broadcast to the screen and speaker on my black box. I might be able to work it out for what you want in a few more months," he added eagerly.

But unaware of Elmer's contradictory equations, all the television viewers within a twenty-five mile radius of Macdonald Hall were wondering why "the Fish" had invaded their homes.

We're looking into it

In her five years as weekend switchboard operator at television station CHUT, Mary Webster had never had such a busy time as on that Sunday evening.

"Everybody wants to know what happened at the end of the Matinee movie," she told her boss, Mr. Tupper. "They're all telling me something about a fish."

"A fish? What are they saying?"

Mary excused herself to answer another call. "CHUT, good evening . . . Oh, yes, madam. John married Louise, and the murderer turned out to be Pierre . . . Yes, madam, I know—a fish. We're looking into it. Thank you for calling CHUT." Mary looked up. "You see? There's another one."

Mr. Tupper frowned. "A fish? What about a fish?"

"They say it appeared, sir," said Mary. "Just at the climax of the movie, the screen showed a big fish. Then there was the most diabolical laughter and someone said, 'Attention, world, we bring you the fish.' Then more laughter. That 'attention, world' business really scared some of our viewers."

"Sounds like a broadcast from outer space," laughed Mr. Tupper. "The invasion of the fish people."

"Go ahead and laugh," she grinned. "But I have to answer the phone. What shall I tell people?"

"Make up something about atmospheric conditions, and tell them we're looking into it," said Mr. Tupper. "That's what we're going to do."

* * *

Elmer Drimsdale's alarm went off with an ear-splitting jangle at six o'clock Monday morning, waking up the three boys in 201 and probably half the dormitory as well.

Elmer threw off the covers and bounded energetically out of bed. He inhaled and exhaled deeply, unable to do his customary deep kneebends because of the lack of space.

"The beginning of another day!" he announced brightly. "Time to tend to all my little friends."

A slipper whizzed by his ear. "Your little friends'll be fine. It's your big friends you've got to worry about," growled Bruno from the depths of his pillow.

Boots sneezed five times, signifying that he was awake for the day. Slowly he began to crawl out of bed.

"Would you like to feed my goldfish?" Elmer offered generously.

"No, thanks," said Boots. "Maybe some other time."

"Perhaps you'd like to sprinkle a little sugar for my ant colony?"

"Oh, all right," sighed Boots. He took the sugar dispenser over to the terrarium, removed the cover and switched on the lamp. He sprinkled a little sugar on top of the sand. Instantly several dozen ants broke to the surface. He sprinkled a little more and more ants emerged. Boots watched, transfixed. "Hey, Bruno," he exclaimed, without taking his eyes from the terrarium, "you should see this. A miniature riot!"

"No, I shouldn't," mumbled Bruno, half asleep.

"Here, you guys," said Boots to the ants. "I'll give you some more."

"No, no," said Elmer quickly. "That's enough for today."

"Yeah," Bruno agreed. "Too much sugar will rot their little teeth."

"You know," said Boots, "that's really neat! I'm going to get me one of these."

"Spare me!" moaned Bruno.

While Boots showered and dressed, Elmer began the long, careful process of watering his plants. Then he too got dressed. Bruno never stirred. Finally, at about 7:15, Boots and Elmer left for the dining hall.

Just as the door clicked behind them, Bruno hopped out of bed and went straight to Elmer's video machine. He switched it on and watched with delight as the salmon materialized on the screen.

"The Fish has arisen," he announced in the deepest voice he could muster. "The Fish is everywhere. Beware the Fish!" He laughed with glee and switched off. This was the best new toy he had had for many a year.

Bruno sighed wistfully. It was too bad Elmer's wonderful machine could not telecast to anything but the little screen on the black box. Bruno would dearly have loved to make his fish jokes via TV to Mr. Sturgeon himself, without the Headmaster's being able to find out it was him.

Little did Bruno know that his message, along with the picture of Elmer's salmon, had reached Mr. Sturgeon—and every other television viewer in the vicinity of Macdonald Hall—by means of the Early Show.

* * *

A class detention made Bruno and Boots late getting out of science class. It was after four when they strolled across the campus towards Dormitory 2.

"Boy, was Mr. Hubert ever mad!" said Bruno. "Who set fire to the counter anyway?"

"Who else?" replied Boots. "Old Butterfingers. But it was an accident."

"With him it always is," grinned Bruno.

The two boys entered the dormitory and walked down the hall to 201. When they opened the door an amazing sight met their eyes. By relocating some furniture and various experiments, Elmer had managed to set up an extensive chemistry laboratory. There was a long table. On it sat a hot plate, two alcohol burners, two pyrex flasks, three dozen test tubes of varying sizes, one high-powered microscope with a stack of slides, and countless little bottles containing chemicals. There were also beakers, eyedroppers, applicator sticks, stirring rods and a scale.

"Elmer, what's going on?" asked Bruno in amazement.

"My cure for the common cold," explained Elmer. "I think I'm on the right track."

"But we have to live here!" Boots protested. "There's no room!"

"Do you know the kind of publicity a cure for the common cold would bring to Macdonald Hall?" cried Bruno enthusiastically. "You go ahead and work, Elm. Take all the room you need!"

"Thank you," mumbled Elmer.

Bruno climbed across Boots's bed and carefully picked his way over to his favourite gadget. He switched it on and waited for the fish image to appear on the screen.

"This is the Fish Patrol," he announced loudly. "We bring you salutations from the fishbowl." He laughed diabolically. "Beware the Fish! You never know where he may strike next." Bruno switched the device off. "Marvellous," he exclaimed. "It's so good for my morale."

"The Fish would kill you if he heard all that," observed Boots.

"How can he hear it?" scoffed Bruno. "We're our own little TV station—one camera, one set"—he pointed to the salmon poster—"and one superstar."

In the Headmaster's residence an annoyed Mrs. Sturgeon, her favourite soap opera rudely interrupted by yet another fish broadcast, was dialling station CHUT.

* * *

At RCMP Headquarters in Ottawa, Deputy Chief Bullock sifted through a pile of memos and reports before leaving for the day. One in particular caught his attention.

Request received from Board of Broadcast Governors to investigate unexplained interruption of TV broadcasts in Chutney, Ontario, Station CHUT. Picture of fish, accompanied by veiled threats and unrelated commentary, blocking regular broadcasts at irregular intervals. Special Division suspects possible development of terrorist activity. Local residents becoming alarmed.

"A picture of a fish?" Deputy Chief Bullock muttered in disbelief. He swivelled in his chair, found Chutney on his map, then sat back in perplexity. Why Chutney?

"Probably a joke," he decided. Still, if it was something serious and he ignored it . . . A smile spread across his face. Sergeant Harold P. Featherstone, assigned to his division just two weeks before, was young, eager and in need of field experience. And he had twice stolen his superior's parking space at Headquarters. Deputy Chief Bullock flipped on the intercom.

"Send Sergeant Featherstone to my office," he told his secretary. "I have an assignment for him."

* * *

"Okay, you guys," announced Bruno, consulting his watch, "it's after midnight. Time to go to Scrimmage's."

"Bruno, are you crazy?" Boots protested. "The Fish said—"

"The Fish said he never wants to catch us over there again," finished Bruno. "If anyone catches us, which isn't due for another million years, it'll be Miss Scrimmage. So let's go."

Their discussion was interrupted by loud, angry voices from down the hall. Boots crawled across his bed and opened the door just in time to see Sidney Rampulsky tearing towards him, trying to outrun a broken lamp that Larry Wilson had thrown at him. Sidney hit the bed and catapulted into the room. He came to rest in a tangle of TV wires and cables.

"And don't come back!" bellowed Larry from 204.

The door of room 200 burst open and Housemaster Alex Flynn, the school's athletic director, rushed out into the hall in his underwear. "Pipe down out here!" he hollered. "It's the middle of the night!" He stormed back into his room and slammed the door.

Bruno helped Sidney up off the floor. "What are you

doing here?" he asked.

"Larry threw me out," complained Sidney. "Gee, he's crabby. It was just an accident."

"*Another* accident?" said Boots. "What did you break this time?"

"His lamp," admitted Sidney. "It fell when I overturned the desk on his foot." He looked anxiously at the three faces around him. "Well, don't look at me like that. Anyone can have a little run of bad luck."

"We have an appointment," said Bruno. "You'll have to go back to your own room."

"But Larry won't let me in!" protested Sidney. "He's really mad!"

"Well, we can't leave you here or you'll wreck the place. You'll just have to come with us to Scrimmage's. There's always room for one more."

"I'll stay here," offered Elmer quickly. "I wouldn't want to jeopardize the expedition. Four people may be noticed more easily than three."

"Good thinking," replied Bruno. "All right, Elm. You stay here and mind the store. Boots, Sidney, let's go."

Bruno and Boots climbed easily out the window and stood flush against the wall. Sidney tumbled out after them, going head over heels across the sill and landing flat on his back in the shrubbery.

Boots flashed his roommate a look of hopelessness as the two of them picked Sidney up. They hustled him across the campus, and with only one further mishap, when he caught his foot in the fence, they finally reached Miss Scrimmage's. Cathy and Diane were already at the window. Pushing Sidney ahead of them, Bruno and Boots climbed up the drainpipe and into the room.

"Hi," Cathy greeted them. "Who's your friend?"

"This is Butterfingers Rampulsky," Bruno said. "He breaks things a lot—usually his own neck."

The girls greeted Sidney in a friendly manner.

"What happened to you two?" Diane asked. "Miss Scrimmage said she turned you over to The Fish. He must have been boiling!"

"Oh, he was," replied Bruno, "but mostly at Miss Scrimmage. He went easy on us—we just got a day's confinement."

"How did you people do with those suggestions?" asked Boots. "How do we make the Hall famous?"

"Most of the girls are pretty stupid," said Cathy. "They suggest that you rob a bank and stuff like that. Then when you get caught you'll get your names in the paper."

"Small minds think alike," Bruno muttered. "We got a lot of that from the guys too. Don't tell me that's the best you can do."

"Not to worry," she announced brightly, "because I, Catherine Elizabeth Burton, using my very own personal brain, thought up the idea that's the answer to your problem."

"What is it?"

"Not so fast," said Cathy, smiling broadly. "What's in it for me?"

"Our undying thanks," said Bruno.

"And a potted philodendron," added Boots, "courtesy of Elmer Drimsdale."

"It's a deal. Here's my idea. If you guys could set a world record at something you'd get into the papers and on TV—and you'd get Macdonald Hall into the *Rankin Book of World Records*."

"That's a great idea!" exclaimed Bruno. "We've got so much talent at the Hall, it'll be a cinch!"

"I agree," said Sidney shyly.

"I don't know," objected Boots. "People who make the record books are mighty hard to beat. Like roller-skating, for instance. The world record holder skated all the way from Victoria to St. John's, almost eight thousand kilometres. I can just see The Fish allowing us to do something like that."

Cathy looked crestfallen. "Do I still get my philodendron?"

"You sure do," said Bruno enthusiastically. "We'll find something we can set a record at. Thanks a million!" He turned to the others. "All right, men, let's go."

"Wait a minute," Diane interrupted. "Don't you want me to get you some food?"

"We don't need any more, thanks," Bruno declined. "We've got our snack back. I think The Fish was shamed when he caught us with a food parcel from here. Anyway, thanks a lot for the idea. We'll be back with your philodendron."

Bruno and Boots swung themselves over the sill and began to climb down the pipe. Sidney followed them.

"He's not so clumsy," Cathy commented to Diane.

Suddenly they heard an all-too-familiar voice.

"Halt!"

The two girls ran to the window and leaned out. Bruno and Boots stood below, illuminated in the beam of Miss Scrimmage's flashlight. Sidney, still undetected, was only part way down.

"What'll we do?" whispered Diane.

"I know. I'll create a diversion." Cathy was always at her best in an emergency. She inhaled, reared back and burst into loud, sustained shrieking.

Startled, Sidney lost his grip on the drainpipe and fell a full seven feet, landing on Miss Scrimmage. Her shotgun and flashlight flew into the air.

Sidney scrambled to his feet and ran, leaving Miss Scrimmage in a heap screaming, "Assault! Assault!" Bruno and Boots tore off after him, the Headmistress's shouts and Cathy's screams ringing in their ears. The three boys did not stop running until they were safe in the bushes under the window of room 201.

Elmer helped the three gasping boys into the room. "What in the world happened?" he asked.

Bruno was the first to find his voice. "I don't believe it!" he said, outraged. "She did it again! She caught me!

Me! Who does she think she is?"

"She thinks she's dead," gasped Boots. "Or attacked anyway. Bruno, she thinks we *attacked* her!"

Bruno ignored him. "That was some quick thinking, Sidney. You really saved our skins! What loyalty! What self-sacrifice!"

"Yeah," said Sidney uncertainly. He rubbed his tailbone. "But I think I hurt myself."

"Are you going to be punished?" said Elmer, horrified.

"No," said Bruno.

"Yes," said Boots.

"Either way," said Bruno, "we've got a lot of work ahead of us. A world record, remember?"

"We might have one already," snapped Boots. "Most times caught by a crazy lady with a shotgun. Will that do?"

"Don't rub it in," moaned Bruno. "I've suffered enough. Sidney, Larry must be asleep by now. Go home so we can all get to bed. But first . . . " He walked over to Elmer's video machine.

* * *

"Calm down, Miss Scrimmage," said Mr. Sturgeon into the telephone. "I can't understand a word you're saying . . . Yes, that's better . . . My boys *attacked* you? *Physically*? . . . Impossible! My boys are capable of a lot of mischief, but not that . . . Miss Scrimmage, I'm very sorry you were assaulted, but no one from Macdonald Hall

46

would do such a thing. No one! . . . Yes, well, since you put it that way, I suppose I *am*, in a way, calling you a liar. I do beg your pardon. Goodnight."

He went to the living room and sat down. "Mildred, you simply won't believe what that ridiculous woman has accused us of this time!"

"What is it, William?" she prompted.

"She says that a whole gang of our boys were over there terrorizing her tender young ladies, and when she caught them they jumped on her and beat her up!"

"That's not possible," exclaimed Mrs. Sturgeon. "Not one of our boys would do such a thing! It's barbaric!"

"If it happened at all," said the Headmaster grimly. "Personally I think Miss Scrimmage has been acting a little peculiar lately." He glanced at the dark television set. "How was the Late Show, Mildred?"

"Oh, I had to turn it off," she said in annoyance. "That dreadful fish was back again."

Room 13

The town of Chutney, population 3100, is located on Highway 48 seven miles north of Macdonald Hall. It has the usual doctor, dentist, police station, undertaker and combination motel-gas station. It also has, on the main street, television station CHUT, serving Chutney and surrounding territory.

It was early Tuesday morning. In room 13 of the Chutney Motel, Sergeant Harold P. Featherstone, Junior, of the Royal Canadian Mounted Police had already cut himself twice trying to shave with cold water. Finally, in disgust, he towelled the shaving cream off his face, left the bathroom and switched on the TV. He was just in time for the morning news.

The black and white picture was of poor quality—and he just might have to watch it all day, he reflected glumly. Deputy Chief Bullock had assigned him to investigate some reports about a strange fish that people in the area were seeing on their screens. Special Division thought it might be the work of a terrorist group. More likely someone playing a joke, Featherstone muttered to himself. But that was before he saw the Fish.

It happened at 8:45. Suddenly the newcaster's face was replaced by the large fuzzy image of a fish. A loud voice shouted, *The Fish Revolution has begun! The Fish is everywhere! Beware the Fish!*, followed by maniacal laughter. Then the newscaster returned.

Shocked, Featherstone reached quickly for a pad and pencil.

* * *

Bruno Walton flicked the switch, deactivating Elmer's machine. "Love it!" he exclaimed, dressing like a whirl-wind. It was his custom not to get out of bed before 8:45, and being on time for nine o'clock classes was not easy.

"C'mon, hurry up," Boots prodded, waiting at the door. "We don't want to be on report. The Fish is proba-bly mad enough at us for last night. When I think of what Sidney did to Miss Scrimmage . . . "

"He didn't do anything," objected Bruno. "It was just an accident. Cathy shouldn't have screamed like that."

"Cathy was just creating a diversion to help us get away. It was quick thinking."

"It was definitely quick," agreed Bruno, pulling a T-shirt over his head, "but I'm not sure it was thinking. Anyway, Miss Scrimmage doesn't know it was us. Let's go. What are you waiting for?"

The two boys ran off to class.

* * *

"Men," said Bruno over the lunch table, "I now call upon your powers of ingenuity to save Macdonald Hall."

"Cut the drivel," snarled Wilbur Hackenschleimer. Ever since the school's austerity program had begun he had been in an indescribably foul mood. "What is it you want us to do this time?"

Bruno was undaunted. "We've decided that the best way to bring publicity to the Hall is to get ourselves into the *Rankin Book of World Records*." He slammed a thick paperback book onto his tray. "Here's the book. All we have to do is take a record and beat it. Do I have a volunteer?"

There was absolute silence.

"I'm very disappointed in you," said Bruno. "Okay, let the bulldozers come and flatten everything! Let them pave our lawn and put up a parking lot! I'm the only guy who cares, and I can't do it by myself!"

"Oh, Bruno, shut up!" sighed Boots. "We'd like to save the school, but world records are hard to break. I was going to go to the Chutney Fair and try to break the record for riding the ferris wheel. Then I looked it up and found out that the guys who hold it rode for more than four weeks! I can just see me asking The Fish for four weeks off school so I can go ride a ferris wheel!"

50

"Hey, I know," said Pete Anderson brightly. "Wilbur could set an eating record. Anything anybody else can eat he can eat more of."

"I'm out of training," Wilbur replied sadly. "I haven't had a square meal in so long that my stomach is probably shrunk down to nothing."

"How about apple peeling?" suggested Sidney Rampulsky. "When Chris Talbot peels an apple he peels it all in one piece and so thin that one time I'll bet it was more than ten feet long!"

Bruno riffled through the book. "Apple peeling—here it is." His face fell. "The longest apple peel is one hundred and seventy-two feet. Chris is a little short."

"How about showering?" asked Larry Wilson. "Perry Elbert spends half his life in the shower. Mort says that when Perry gets upset he gets into the shower and stays there half the day."

Boots grabbed the record book and turned to the appropriate listing. "No good," he said. "It says here the record is something like eight days. Not even Perry could get that upset."

"Read us some," Pete suggested, "and we'll see if they can be done."

Boots handed the book back to Bruno, who thumbed the pages. "Let's see—gold panning, grape catching, grave digging, guitar playing..."

"Boots could do that," said Sidney.

"I don't think so," answered Bruno glumly. "He'd

have to play for more than a hundred and eleven hours and fifteen minutes to beat the record. I don't think The Fish would be too thrilled with that. And the teachers wouldn't be so happy about having their classes set to music either." He turned a few pages. "Let's see. What else is there? Piano smashing, plate spinning, pogo stick jumping . . ."

"I could do that," offered Sidney. "I'm really good with a pogo stick."

There was general laughter, punctuated by Larry's snort of disgust.

"If you can beat forty-two thousand hops in six hours and six minutes, speak up," said Bruno. "Hmmm—pole sitting. Let's see . . . Forget it. The record is two hundred and seventy-three days."

He flipped another couple of pages. "Hey, look at this! The biggest ball of string is four metres in diameter—no, we haven't got enough time to collect something like that. How about talking? No, a hundred and thirty-eight hours is a little too long. The Fish wouldn't allow it. If it weren't for The Fish, you know, we could set all kinds of wonderful records!"

He glanced down the page. "Hot gazoobies, this is it! Tin can pyramid! The record is a pyramid with a base almost eight feet square. It was fifteen feet high and used twenty-two thousand one hundred and forty pop cans. The base was forty cans by forty cans." He whistled. "That's pretty good, but we can beat it. We'll make one with a base forty-five cans square. Elmer?"

Elmer chewed thoughtfully on a dried fig. "Such a structure," he said, "would be seventeen feet eight inches high with a base eight feet ten inches square, based on the dimensions of an average soda-pop can. We would require thirty-one thousand three hundred and ninety-five cans."

"No sweat!" exclaimed Bruno. "Everywhere you look there's a pop can lying around."

"The Chutney dump must be full of them," added Wilbur. "And if we can't find enough there, there must be millions around Toronto."

"In this case," said Boots, "the litterbug is our best friend."

"If we can get everyone in the school scavenging for pop cans, and all the girls at Scrimmage's too, we can get enough."

"We'd have to go off campus," warned Boots. "And we can't have everybody requesting leave on the same day. I take it we don't want The Fish to know about this."

"You take it right," agreed Bruno. "He'd probably tell us to stop our foolishness and concentrate on our studies. The way I see it, we can all walk to Chutney Friday night and from there we'll catch buses all over the place —Gormley, Stouffville, Uxbridge—and a lot of us can even go into Toronto. We'll all trickle back sometime

Saturday."

There was a wild babble of protest.

Bruno stood up and pounded the table. "All right, you guys, I know it's risky, but there's safety in numbers. The Fish won't be able to expel all six hundred of us. And if we don't do it, then we might as well go home anyway because pretty soon there won't be any Macdonald Hall."

The protest died.

"How about this?" challenged Boots. "Where are we going to keep thirty thousand pop cans?"

"I thought of that already," replied Bruno smugly. "We can hide them in Dormitory 3. Nobody even goes near there since they closed it up. It's the perfect place." He paused. "Well, what do you think?"

"Let's do it," said Pete. "We've got nothing to lose that we won't lose in the long run anyway."

The other boys at the table murmured their agreement.

"Good," said Bruno. "We've got until Friday to spread the word. I want every kid in this school to know what's expected of him. Tell them we're aiming for sixty cans per person—more if they can manage it." He grinned with satisfaction. "Don't worry. We'll pull it off."

The boys began to file out en route to their afternoon classes.

*   *   *

Sergeant Harold P. Featherstone, Junior, was watching television. As a matter of fact, except for a twenty minute lunch break at Willy's Hamburger Emporium and half an hour for dinner at the diner across the road, he had been watching television all day. Disappointingly, there had been no fish broadcast since 8:45 that morning.

He lay down on the bed with his tape recorder to make his report. "Investigation Fish," he began, "Field Report Number One—Sergeant Harold P. Featherstone, Special Division, reporting."

He recorded the details of the 8:45 incident, and then wracked his brain for something else to say.

"I am convinced," he continued, unsuccessfully suppressing a yawn, "that something very significant may be taking place here. The Fish—uh—as it were—may be . . ." His voice trailed off and he fell asleep, snoring gently. The tape continued to turn, recording his peaceful slumber.

Next door in room 14, a tall, cadaverous man crouched with his ear pressed against the wall, trying in vain to hear what was being said in Featherstone's room.

* * *

"Bruno, Boots—you guys must be crazy to come here after what happened the last two times!" exclaimed Diane Grant as the two Macdonald Hall boys entered through the window.

"Is the old girl all right?" asked Bruno.

"Oh, she's fine," said Cathy. "Don't worry about Miss Scrimmage. She's immortal. Mad, too. When she called to complain, The Fish didn't believe her."

"So *that's* how come we got away with it! Anyway, here's your philodendron." Boots placed a potted plant on the desk.

Bruno laughed. "At first Elmer was reluctant to part with one of his little friends. But we told him either to fork it over or come here and personally explain to you why you couldn't have it. After that he donated it with an open heart. You really made an impression on him."

"We try," said Cathy modestly. "What's happening with the world records?"

"Plenty," replied Boots. "Bruno's got the whole school in an uproar over it."

"Terrific," exclaimed Cathy. "I love uproars. Can we help?"

"Yes," said Bruno, "as a matter of fact, you can. We're going for the world's largest pop-can pyramid record and we need some cans."

"How many?" asked Diane.

"Oh, no more than thirty-two thousand," said Bruno casually.

"Sure," retorted Cathy sarcastically. "No problem. To-morrow I'll just stroll out and pick up thirty-two thousand pop cans. Simplicity itself."

"Listen," insisted Bruno, exasperated, "just tell the girls to get all the pop cans they can find."

"As it happens, you've picked a good time. The whole school is going to the Ontario Art Gallery on Saturday —or so Miss Scrimmage thinks."

"Cathy!" Diane protested. "We can't—"

"We can and we will," was Cathy's reply. "And Miss Scrimmage can't expel us because we're taking the whole school along. There's strength in numbers."

Boots cast Bruno a strange look. He had heard that philosophy before.

"Right," said Bruno. "You girls should be able to pick up a lot of cans in a city the size of Toronto. Keep them for us and we'll get them on Saturday night."

"So we won't be seeing you for a while," said Diane with a mixture of regret and hope.

"Right," agreed Boots. "Goodnight." As he swung a leg over the sill, his shoe came off and fell to the ground with a thud.

"Halt!" cried a voice, and they could see the beam of a flashlight below.

"Oh, no!" moaned Bruno, yanking Boots away from the window. "It's her again! What does she want from me?"

"Your neck," snapped Boots. "And mine."

"She'll be up here in a minute. We'd better get you guys to sanctuary." Cathy bustled them out into the corridor and knocked on the next door. A tall, red-haired girl opened up and peered out.

"Hi, Ruth," greeted Cathy genially. "Would you hide

these for us? We'll be back for them soon." She shoved Bruno and Boots into the room, shut the door and re-entered her own room.

"Hi, Ruth," said Bruno conversationally. "I'm Bruno, he's Boots."

The girl grinned. "I've heard about you two. The sleeping beauty over there," she indicated her slumbering roommate, "is Wilma Dorf."

There were quick footsteps in the hall. "And the avenging angel out there," whispered Bruno, "is Miss Scrimmage. What have you got in the way of a listening device?"

Ruth reached into the bathroom and handed him a drinking glass. Bruno put his ear to the glass and the glass to the wall just in time to hear Cathy say, "Oh, Miss Scrimmage, they were back! They were bothering us!"

"Never mind, dear," comforted the Headmistress. "I chased them away. But I've got them *this* time. One of them left his shoe behind. Now that old goat—uh—now Mr. Sturgeon will have to admit that I am right and that his boys have been harassing us."

"Miss Scrimmage, you're so clever!" exclaimed Cathy.

"I do what I must," replied Miss Scrimmage modestly. "Now you two go to sleep. Young ladies must have their rest."

Bruno heard the door click, and then more footsteps in the hall. In a few seconds Cathy was tapping at the door.

Ruth opened it.

"Thanks a lot," said Cathy. "I hope they weren't too much trouble. They're very mischievous, you know."

"It's their age," grinned Ruth. "Goodnight."

Cathy ushered them back into her room, where they found Diane white as a sheet. "Cathy, how could you say all that with a straight face?" she asked, aghast. "Don't you get *scared*?"

Cathy laughed. "Of Miss Scrimmage? Never!" She turned to Bruno and Boots. "I'm afraid you'll have to stick around for a while. I think Miss Scrimmage is going over to Mr. Sturgeon's house with Boots's shoe. If she sees you two walking across the campus she'll blast you to kingdom come!"

"My shoe!" moaned Boots. "The Fish'll know it's mine!"

"Don't be an idiot," soothed Bruno. "It's just a sneaker, that's all."

"I know," said Cathy brightly. "Nothing livens up a dull evening like food. Diane, see what you can find in the kitchen."

* * *

It was after 1 A.M. when Mr. Sturgeon answered the insistant ringing of his doorbell. He opened the door to find Miss Scrimmage standing there, indignation written all over her face.

"Your gang of marauders was back tonight!" she accused. "I scared them away."

"I see," said Mr. Sturgeon cautiously. "I trust they didn't harm you?"

"No, I'm fine, thank you," the Headmistress replied. She waved Boots's tennis shoe under his nose. "One of them left this behind. A significant clue, wouldn't you say?"

Mr. Sturgeon smiled thinly. "Miss Scrimmage, that shoe could very well belong to one of your girls."

Miss Scrimmage stiffened. "Young ladies do not have feet of such gargantuan proportions," she retorted icily. "I want you to have a bed-check immediately. And every boy at Macdonald Hall must be made to try on this shoe. That way we shall discover who one of the terrorists is."

Mr. Sturgeon did something he seldom did. He laughed out loud. "Miss Scrimmage," he replied finally, still chuckling, "this is a school, not a twentieth century version of Cinderella. May I suggest that you go home and sleep it off. No doubt things will look brighter in the morning. Goodnight."

Miss Scrimmage turned around and marched off in a huff.

Mrs. Sturgeon appeared at her husband's elbow.

"Mildred," he said, "wait till you hear *this*!"

"I heard," she sighed. "Cinderella."

He nodded. "Mildred, if things go badly and we do lose Macdonald Hall, my one consolation will be that I'll never have to put up with *her* again!"

* * *

60

Elmer pulled Bruno and Boots in through the window of room 201. "Where have you been? It's after three!"

Bruno cast Elmer a look that could have melted lead, and hurled himself onto his bed without a word.

"You'll have to excuse him," Boots explained with a grin. "Miss Scrimmage was out there again and he's having a confidence crisis."

"I don't know," Bruno growled. "It's getting to be so a guy can't sneak out after lights-out any more. What's going on around here anyway?"

Boots shrugged and began to prepare for bed.

"I have some news," offered Elmer timidly. "My cure for the common cold is ready to be tested."

Miraculously restored, Bruno jumped up. "Hot gazoobies! We'll do that tomorrow! Who do we know with a cold?"

"Nobody," said Boots. "None of the guys have colds right now. It's not the cold season."

"Surely *somebody* has a cold," insisted Bruno.

Across the hall in room 200, Housemaster Flynn went into a spasm of violent sneezing. He could be heard rustling around, clearing his throat and blowing his nose.

Bruno and Boots exchanged looks of pure delight.

An uncommon cure

Good morning, all! The Fish launches Operation Popcan! Beware the Fish!

Sergeant Featherstone noted with some excitement that Wednesday morning's announcement also came at 8:45. When the fish disappeared, he switched off the television set. His mind reeling with ideas and suspicions, he turned on his tape recorder.

"Investigation Fish—Field Report Number Two—Sergeant Harold P. Featherstone, Special Division, reporting," he dictated.

"A pattern is beginning to emerge. There have been Fish broadcasts reported at all hours of the day, but 8:45 A.M. seems to be standard. It is my suspicion that 'the Fish' is a code name for the leader of a terrorist cell which is using public communications to send messages, also possibly in code. This morning 'Operation Popcan' was announced. This could be a major manoeuvre planned by the Fish and his associates. I will have to be extremely alert and watchful.

"Featherstone out."

He switched off the recorder, and responding to a rumble in his stomach, left his room in search of breakfast.

The door of the next room opened slightly and two eyes watched intently as Featherstone walked through the parking lot to the street and across to the diner. Then the tall thin man in room 14 also left the motel and casually headed for the little restaurant.

*   *   *

"And that's the way I expect you to complete the obstacle course," said Coach Flynn, jumping off the climbing apparatus in the gymnasium. "Any questions?" He sneezed violently.

Bruno elbowed Boots in the ribs. Boots raised his hand.

"Sir, I have a question about the vaulting horse in the far corner. Isn't there too much space between it and the springboard? Could we take a closer look?"

Flynn took Boots and the rest of the class over to the far corner of the gym. Bruno stole away from the group and moved swiftly to the bench where Coach Flynn kept his glass of Muscle-Ade, a high-energy drink. From the pocket of his shorts he took out the eye-dropper bottle of cold remedy that Elmer had given him. Holding the dropper over the coach's glass, he administered exactly six drops, as per instructions. Then he strolled back and merged with the group. Boots's problem had apparently been cleared up.

The coach again sneezed violently. "Oh, this cold!" he groaned. "I've got a beaut!"

"Maybe some Muscle-Ade will help," suggested Bruno hopefully. "People with colds should drink a lot."

"Good idea," agreed Flynn. He jogged over to the bench, picked up the glass and drained it.

Boots shut his eyes.

A strange look came over Flynn's face.

"Funny," he said. "It never tasted like that before." He hiccupped, took three faltering steps and collapsed to the floor, where he began to snore loudly.

Boots opened his eyes and took in the scene with a gasp of horror. "Bruno, we've killed him!"

"He isn't dead," declared Bruno. "He's just asleep. Funny, Elmer didn't mention that he was going to fall asleep."

"What happened?" cried Pete Anderson. "I'd better go get The Fish!"

"No! No Fish!" shouted Bruno. "No Fish!"

"Fish," murmured Flynn. A goofy grin spread over his face and he began to giggle softly, still asleep.

"What'll we do?" asked Rob Adams nervously.

"We'd better take him home to bed," Bruno decided.

"How are we going to get him all the way to Dormitory 2 without anybody noticing?" demanded Boots, slightly hysterical.

"If we all crowd around him," explained Bruno, "we can walk him all the way." He looked at the rest of the class. "You guys with us?"

"Gee, I don't know," said Chris Talbot uncertainly.

"Well," said Bruno, "if we don't get him out of here, you guys will have to share the blame when The Fish catches us."

"I'm not sure, but I think that's blackmail," commented someone.

"Gee, I didn't even do anything and I'm in trouble!"

"What did you do to him?"

"Was it poison?"

"Poisoned guys don't snore, stupid. They die."

"Let's get him out of here!"

Bruno and Boots hoisted their coach to his feet, supporting him under each arm. All the boys crowded around and in a body walked him across the campus to Dormitory 2. Flynn sang *The Maple Leaf Forever* all the way.

"My, he's patriotic," chuckled Bruno as they crowded down the hall to room 200.

"Yes, and he's also heavy!" panted Boots. "Open the door!"

Bruno plucked the key from Flynn's jacket pocket and unlocked the door.

"*In days of yore,*" sang Flynn as the rest of the boys beat a hasty retreat, leaving Bruno and Boots to tend to their coach. They dragged him across the room and dropped him on his bed.

"Paper," ordered Bruno. "Get paper."

"We don't need paper! We need an ambulance!" said Boots frantically.

"It's almost lunch time," insisted Bruno. "Elmer will explain everything. Meanwhile we've got to put a sign on the gym door saying that afternoon classes are cancelled because the coach has a bad cold. See to it."

"But, Bruno, what if—?"

"It's a beautiful day," shouted Flynn, throwing his arms and legs in the air.

"He's not sick," insisted Bruno. "You can see that. I don't know what he is, but he isn't sick. Let's make that sign and go meet Elmer in the dining room."

"Hey, you guys," mumbled Flynn, "don't go. The party's just getting started."

Boots shot Bruno a worried look as they left the room. After a short detour to place the sign explaining Flynn's absence on the gymnasium door, Bruno and Boots caught up with Elmer Drimsdale at the entrance to the dining hall.

"Elmer, we have to talk to you!" said Bruno.

Elmer gazed at him questioningly.

"Your stupid cold cure!" cried Boots. "It poisoned the coach!"

"Impossible," said Elmer. "There is no toxic material in my formula."

"Then why did he pass out?" cried Boots.

Elmer cocked his head. "He shouldn't have. Perhaps it's all psychological. Did you explain to him that it's completely harmless?"

"Not exactly," replied Bruno. "We slipped it into his Muscle-Ade."

"Oh, dear!" said Elmer. "There's the reason. Muscle-Ade has citric acid. My formula should not be taken with citric acid."

"What happens?" gasped Boots.

"There is a reaction," explained Elmer, "rather similar to the ingestion of large quantities of alcoholic beverages."

"Elmer, speak English!" Bruno snapped.

"Mr. Flynn is drunk," translated Elmer.

Bruno and Boots sat down on the ground and laughed, mostly with relief.

"Perhaps we had better attend to him," suggested Elmer. "This will, of course, wear off in a few hours, but it would never do if someone saw him in this condition. After all, it is your fault."

"*Our* fault?" objected Bruno as they began hurrying to Dormitory 2. "It was your concoction that got him bombed!"

"It was administered incorrectly," accused Elmer primly.

They entered the dormitory and ran down the hall. The door of room 200 was open. Flynn was gone.

"Oh, no!" moaned Boots, leaning against the wall for support.

"Oh, no!" repeated Bruno. "If we don't find him before The Fish sees him, we'll have to confess!"

"Oh, no!" echoed Elmer. "Where could he have gone?"

"If you were a drunk gym teacher, where would you go?" demanded Bruno.

"I would stay home where I wouldn't worry my students!" muttered Boots feelingly.

"We have to get him back to his room!" Bruno said. "Elmer, check the gym. Boots, you look in his office in the Faculty Building. I'll take the staff dining room. Come on, let's move!"

The three boys ran out of Dormitory 2 and were about to go off on their separate errands when, across the road, Miss Scrimmage's outdoor public address system sprang to life.

"*Oh, give me a home where the buffalo roam,*" sang a male voice loudly and rather off-key.

"Flynn!" chorused Bruno and Boots, horrified.

As Flynn finished his song, a voice they recognized as Cathy Burton's howled, "*One more time!*"

Obediently, Flynn began again.

Finally Cathy's voice returned. "*Attention out there.*"

"*You tell 'em!*" cheered Flynn.

"*We have a stray here,*" Cathy continued. "*He's tall, red-haired, and answers to the name of Al. Would someone please come to claim him immediately.*"

As Bruno and Boots rushed towards Scrimmage's, a nervous Elmer Drimsdale stumbling along behind them, they could see a group of girls escorting their coach down the driveway to the side of the road. The boys ran up to them.

"Is Miss Scrimmage around?" Boots asked anxiously. "Did she see him?"

"Yes and no," offered Cathy. "When he walked into her sitting room and asked her to dance, she fainted." She turned to Flynn. "Okay, Al, it's time for you to go home now."

"Don't want to go," said Flynn sulkily. "Like it here."

"Come again any time, Al," said Cathy genially. " 'Bye."

Bruno, Boots and Elmer hustled Flynn across the road and across the campus to Dormitory 2. Luckily, they attracted very little attention from the student body and were not seen by any member of the staff.

"Please, Coach," begged Boots as they placed Flynn on his bed, "please have a nap."

"I know! Let's play cards!" Flynn suggested brightly.

"We can't, sir," said Elmer. "We have classes this afternoon."

"Then why are you wasting my time?" cried Flynn, starting for the door. "I'm going back to that Scrimmage place! Asked a lady to dance . . . "

"Cards it is!" said Bruno quickly.

"Good! Didn't like her anyway." Flynn rummaged through a drawer for a deck of cards.

Bruno noticed Elmer quietly sneaking out the door. "Drimsdale, get back here! You're in this too!"

Red-faced, Elmer slithered back in.

"And just to make it interesting," said Flynn, "we'll play for toothpicks."

They all sat down on the floor and began to play poker. In half an hour Flynn was fast asleep and Elmer had won all the toothpicks.

"Beginner's luck," mumbled Bruno. They tiptoed out, careful not to waken their sleeping coach.

* * *

"Miss Scrimmage," Mr. Sturgeon snapped into his office telephone, "you have made up stories before, but this one is beyond anything! No member of my staff was over at your school running about in his underwear! They were all in class except my athletic director who spent the afternoon in bed with a bad cold! ... Yes, I am sure! As a matter of fact, I am positive! ... My staff does not drink during school hours, and none of them ever drinks to excess! ... Miss Scrimmage, it simply cannot have happened! ... No, I was not watching Mr. Flynn a hundred percent of the time! ... Mr. Flynn is an athlete! He does not smoke or drink! He won't even eat fried foods! ... Miss Scrimmage ... Miss Scrimmage ... ?"

The Headmaster buzzed his secretary. "Mrs. Davis, I'll

be out for a few moments."

He left the Faculty Building and walked to Dormitory 2, going straight to room 200 and tapping at the door. There was no answer. From inside he could hear loud snoring.

He shook his head. "That woman!" he said aloud. He strode back to his office.

* * *

"Investigation Fish—Field Report Number Three—Sergeant Harold P. Featherstone, Special Division, reporting," dictated Sergeant Featherstone into his tape recorder. He was locked in the motel bathroom and had the shower, sink and fan all running.

"A further development has arisen," he continued softly. "I am being followed by a tall, thin, dark-haired man with a long nose. He is staying in the room next to mine. Everywhere I go, he goes. I am reporting from my bathroom with the water running to render any bugging devices ineffective. I suspect he is one of the Fish's operatives, or perhaps the Fish himself. Whichever, it is obvious that the Fish knows of my presence here in Chutney. I will take all necessary precautionary measures.

"Featherstone out."

Operation popcan

Friday night after lights-out, few students were in bed.
The woods behind Macdonald Hall were crawling with
boys, all setting out on the great pop-can round-up. Most
of the boys had had the same idea—to take to the woods
until they were out of sight of the school and then cut
over to the highway for the long walk to Chutney.

Bruno and Boots trudged along behind Larry and Sidney.

"How come you're going, Larry?" asked Bruno. "What
if The Fish needs a messenger tomorrow and you're not
back yet?"

"I'm just going as far as the drive-in movie outside
Chutney," Larry replied. "Pete and Wilbur are already
there. Sidney'll go on with them, and I'll go home with
the cans from the drive-in." He squinted in the dark.
"Say, where's Elmer?"

"He's staying home," explained Boots. "He said something about a remote-control thingamajig he's working on."

"Where are you guys going?" asked Sidney.

"Oh, we're going to Toronto," Bruno said airily.

Boots was worried. "Bruno, Toronto is awfully far. I thought we'd just sort of hang around Chutney."

"If everyone just sort of hangs around Chutney," pointed out Bruno, "we won't get enough cans, will we?"

Boots fell silent. He had decided quite a while earlier that the entire pop-can project was ridiculous and rather out of reach, but from long experience he knew there was no point in telling this to Bruno Walton, who had his heart and mind set on it. Boots found himself wondering what Mr. Sturgeon would do if he discovered that ninety percent of his students had walked out in the middle of the night.

His thoughts were shared by many of the boys who trudged north on Highway 48 that night. They walked, for the most part, in silence.

* * *

"Hey, look at this!" exclaimed Rob Adams as he and his companion, Marvin Trimble, boarded the 10 P.M. bus for Richmond Hill. "A pop can right under my seat! This is going to be easier than we thought!" He unfolded a green garbage bag and tossed the can in. "One," he counted.

"We're really on our way," commented Marvin dryly as the bus pulled out.

* * *

Sergeant Harold P. Featherstone, Junior, reclined in the front seat of his old Volkswagen Beetle, sipping the last few drops of a can of ginger ale and watching the late-night movie at the drive-in. His stomach rumbled loudly as he got out of the car and headed for the snack bar.

From out of the darkness Pete Anderson appeared. He reached up for Featherstone's pop can, shook it, and finding it empty, tossed it into his bag. It clanked against many others.

Five minutes later Featherstone returned, carrying a hot dog and another drink. He noticed two things: his pop can had disappeared and the man in the car directly behind him, though disguised in a trench coat, a hat and dark glasses, was unmistakably the mysterious man from room 14. Featherstone was now sure that the long-nosed man was working for the Fish and that Operation Pop-can, whatever it was, had already begun.

* * *

"Nothing in here," echoed Perry Elbert's voice from the depths of a garbage can.

"Don't we have enough?" complained his roommate, Mortimer Day. "Between the two of us, we must have fifty of them."

"Bruno said he wants us to get at least sixty each," said Perry. "That's a hundred and twenty. We're short, but it's early yet."

"Do you mean to tell me that we're going into every garbage can in Chutney?" asked Mort indignantly.

"And maybe Stouffville if we have time."

Mort groaned. "I hate it when Bruno runs things!"

Perry grunted in agreement. "Me too, but this time it's important. We're doing this to save the school."

"I don't see how a pyramid of tin cans, even the largest one in the world, will save the school," objected Mort.

"Neither do I," said Perry, "but everybody's out collecting, so it has to have some point."

"Jackpot!" whispered Mort in sudden delight. "A whole case of empties!"

*   *   *

"This alley is paradise to the pop can hunter!" exclaimed Louis Brown, stuffing cans into his bag with both hands.

"We must have a million by now!" agreed Mark Davies.

"Good. Let's go back before we get into trouble," urged the third member of the group, Gary Potts. "We don't need any more cans."

"After we clean out this alley," said Mark, peering behind some old crates, "we'll talk about it."

"I want to go home!" insisted Gary.

* * *

Chris Talbot and Rodney Stitt had taken a bus all the
way to Gormley because they had discovered that there
was a soft drink manufacturer there. To their utter disap-
pointment, the Gormley Soda Works turned out to be a
bottler. No cans. Their night was saved, however, when
they accidentally stumbled upon the leavings of a very
large company picnic at a park across from the bus
depot. There they amassed over two hundred empty pop
cans between them.

* * *

When the movie ended Featherstone aimed his car towards the one exit, and with a screech of his tires, turned
out onto the highway. In his rear-view mirror he could
see the usual congested traffic leaving the drive-in lot. He
had the satisfaction of knowing that he had left the man
from room 14 far behind in the jam.

* * *

"I don't like this place!" complained Sidney Rampulsky,
on his hands and knees in a pile of rubbish. "It stinks!"

"What did you expect the Chutney dump to smell
like?" demanded Wilbur. "Roses? Anyway, there's a lot
of cans here."

"They stink too," said Sidney. "We're going to have
the smelliest pop-can pyramid in the world."

"Two world records," grunted Wilbur.

Pete Anderson appeared, shining a flashlight over a mountain of trash. "This whole thing makes me nervous," he complained. "What if The Fish comes?"

"The Fish is snug in his bed back at the Hall," said Sidney, "where I wish *I* was. Besides, if he did discover we were missing, I figure the dump is the last place he'd look for us."

"It makes me nervous too," said Wilbur, stuffing a whole pile of cans into his bag. "Sometimes I think we're nuts to do what Bruno tells us."

"Keep picking them up," sighed Sidney. "The sooner we get out of here, the better."

* * *

In search of clues to Operation Popcan, Featherstone cruised along side roads on his way back to the Chutney Motel. Not knowing what one was looking for, he reflected, made an investigation rather difficult. At first he had thought Operation Popcan was only a code name. And yet someone, probably the Fish's agent from room 14, had deliberately gone to his car and stolen his empty pop can. What on earth for? he asked himself. Was there really some sort of strange terrorist activity developing in this peaceful town?

He came to a bend in the road and suddenly caught a glimpse of a dim light up ahead in what appeared to be a field. He drove a little farther, stopped the car and got out. The smell of rotting garbage assailed his nostrils.

The town dump. Someone was foraging around the dump. But why? The dump was full of garbage and refuse and—pop cans.

Gingerly, trying to ignore his racing heart, he stepped over the wire fence and began to creep silently toward the spot where he could still see the light bobbing. Now he could hear several voices. Careful. He was outnumbered.

"I did! I did see a car! It stopped right over there and then the lights went out!"

"*The Fish*!" screeched Pete Anderson, switching off his flashlight. "Let's get out of here!"

Sidney Rampulsky grabbed his two giant bags full of pop cans and ran aimlessly. At the top of a mound his foot got snagged on the edge of an old broken bathtub. The tub rolled over and started a landslide of garbage down the mound. Panic-stricken, Sidney looked down and saw, seven feet below him, a white face with two hands held up in front of it in a futile attempt to ward off the avalanche.

Sidney wheeled and tore off after Wilbur Hackenschleimer's burly, fleeing form. Passing Wilbur and then Pete, he howled, "Let's move! There's a *guy* back there!"

The three, only slightly impeded by the bags they still clutched, ran off into the night. They did not stop until they were halfway back to Macdonald Hall.

* * *

In the Chutney dump a pile of garbage stirred and a head broke the surface. With great effort and much spitting and muttering, Sergeant Featherstone arose and shook himself, spraying garbage everywhere. He stood there for an instant squinting about him and then, with a groan, dropped to his knees in the mess and began foraging. After a few minutes he came up with his glasses. He stumbled away from the dump, eased himself back over the fence and crossed the road to his car. Miserably, he realized that the aroma of rotten garbage had come with him.

He turned the key in the ignition. The engine turned over once, choked and died. He tried again. Same result. And again. He checked the gas gauge. Empty. He tried to picture his police training manual, but could not recall a page dictating what an officer should do when he finds himself covered in garbage, in the middle of nowhere, with an empty gas tank.

He began to walk towards Chutney, passing the time by making a mental list of the many unpleasant things he had in store for the Fish when he apprehended him.

* * *

"*Notice*," read Jim Duffy. "*Beginning September 20th, there will be no transit service between the hours of 1 A.M. and 6 A.M.*"

"Terrific!" exclaimed Fred Johnston, resting his load against the bus shelter. "We're stranded in beautiful downtown Stouffville! Call me a taxi. Or better still, a truck. We can't walk all the way home!"

"We'll just have to wait until six," sighed Jim. "And while we're at it, we may as well pick up a few more cans."

Fred groaned. "Wait till I get my hands on Bruno Walton!"

* * *

Just before dawn a group of fifteen boys crept onto the Macdonald Hall campus, each carrying large bags full of cans. They stole across the lawn to the abandoned Dormitory 3 and opened the main door.

John Oak stepped inside. "Wow!" he whispered admiringly. "Look at this!"

The dormitory hall was lined with neatly-stacked pop cans, already stretching past two doorways. The stacks were four cans high. Their metallic surfaces glinted in the dim moonlight.

"We'll have to stack ours too," John whispered to the others. "That's what everyone else is doing." To set a good example, he began placing his cans one by one in a neat stack with the others.

"How many do you think we've got?" whispered someone.

"About a billion!"

"About five hundred."

"Probably a few thousand."

"A lot more than any normal person would want!"

"My feet are killing me!"

"I don't think we have enough."

"Don't worry. There's lots more coming."

"My feet!"

"Your feet? My back!"

"Shhhhh!"

Their cans all neatly stowed away, the boys headed for their rooms to catch two hours sleep before breakfast.

* * *

Dawn found Bruno Walton and Boots O'Neal in Toronto's High Park because, as Bruno put it, "It's right in the middle of the city. There are picnics, school field trips, office workers having lunch—there must be millions of pop cans!"

And there were. The trash baskets were piled high with the previous day's leavings, since the clean-up crew had not yet come on duty.

"We should have brought more guys!" exclaimed Bruno enthusiastically. "We could get thirty-two thousand cans just from this park!"

"Who else would be stupid enough to come all the way to Toronto?" moaned Boots, yawning hugely. "How are we ever going to get all these cans back to the Hall?"

"Oh, that's the easy part," said Bruno, tossing three cans into his second bag. "Via the Art Gallery at four o'clock."

"Scrimmage's?" asked Boots in horror.

Bruno shrugged. "They're going to have two or three buses. Surely they'll have room for little old us."

"Bruno, we've got two huge bags of junk apiece! How do you figure we can just slip onto one of their buses unnoticed? Miss Scrimmage is bound to catch us!"

"The girls will all have big bags of junk too," said Bruno. "Don't worry. I'll look after everything."

"I'd rather take the bus to Chutney and walk back to the Hall," said Boots hopefully.

"Well, let me put it this way," said Bruno. "We have enough money either for bus fare or for lunch. Take your choice." He smiled engagingly. "And Miss Scrimmage's buses go for free."

* * *

Having spent a full two hours in the bathtub, Sergeant Featherstone then turned on the shower for cover noise and began to record his report.

"Investigation Fish—Field Report Number Four—Sergeant Harold P. Featherstone, Special Division, reporting.

"Last night I managed to elude the Fish's agent from room 14 and pursue my investigation in secrecy. I came upon what I believe to be a phase of Operation Popcan at the Chutney town dump. Several people were involved, descriptions impossible due to poor light. They

82

were using the code word Fish. As I closed in on them, one of the terrorists made a vicious attempt on my life by starting an avalanche of garbage. I got a good look at my assailant, and I must say that I have never seen a more evil face in my entire career. I shall certainly know him when we meet again.

"Featherstone out."

* * *

At mid-morning on Saturday, a group of nine Macdonald Hall students who had met on the way home stole onto the campus from the rear by way of the woods. Taking care to keep out of sight, they eased their way into Dormitory 3 through a side window. In the hallway, a wondrous sight met their eyes: row upon row of neatly-stacked pop cans lined the wall. To their weary souls it was awe-inspiring evidence of great achievement.

"It kind of makes you *believe*, doesn't it?" commented Chris Talbot.

The group began to stack their own cans.

* * *

"All right, girls," said Miss Scrimmage brightly. "Now that your guided tour of the gallery is over, you may spend the next two hours looking over the exhibits that interested you the most. Or perhaps you might enjoy having a small snack in the cafeteria. Your time is your own, but be sure to be back at the buses at quarter to four. Run along, now."

Like a general, Cathy Burton marched the entire population of Miss Scrimmage's school down the hall and into the ladies' room. There each girl was handed a green garbage bag, hoisted out the window to the street and sent in search of pop cans.

After the last girl had been sped on her way, Diane turned to Cathy. "What about us? What are we doing?"

"I'm not fool enough to chase all over town looking for pop cans," replied Cathy. "There must be a million of them right in the cafeteria of this building."

"Gee," chuckled Diane admiringly, "you sure know how to plan the right way."

"I hope so," grinned Cathy. "And I hope the guys build their pyramid and get into the record book. Things would be awfully dull around our place if we lost Macdonald Hall."

* * *

"There are the buses," said Bruno as he and Boots approached the Art Gallery. "All we have to do is sneak aboard and we're home free."

"It's hard to sneak anywhere," observed Boots, "when you're carrying two gigantic bags that clank. Would you mind telling me how we're going to do it?"

"Easy," said Bruno. "We wait for the girls and we all

clank on together."

On cue, a line of girls began to stream out of the building. Bruno and Boots quickly ran over and merged with the crowd. Spotting them, Cathy and Diane pushed their way over.

"Hi," said Cathy. "Want a lift?"

"Yes, please," replied Bruno, grinning.

The line stopped.

"My goodness," said Miss Scrimmage at the entrance to the bus. "Why is everyone carrying such huge parcels?"

"Souvenirs, Miss Scrimmage," piped Bruno, falsetto.

"Oh, how nice!" exclaimed the Headmistress with delight. "I *am* pleased that you all enjoyed the gallery so. Let me have a peek." She looked into the bag carried by the first girl in line and raised a perplexed face. "Uh— splendid," she said dubiously. "All right, now, girls. Everybody on the buses."

They all filed on, Cathy and Diane keeping Bruno and Boots well hidden.

"How strange," commented Miss Scrimmage to the driver. "I counted two more than we brought."

The driver shrugged indifferently. "They're probably from the other bus," he said.

"Yes," she agreed. "I guess that's it."

Both buses pulled away from the Art Gallery.

Bruno thoroughly enjoyed the trip, hanging his head out the window to catch the breeze. Boots, on the other hand, sat in hunched misery, hiding his face in his green garbage bags and peeking out now and then to check the back of Miss Scrimmage's head.

When the buses finally pulled into the driveway of Miss Scrimmage's Finishing School for Young Ladies, Bruno turned to Cathy.

"You'll have to take our stuff," he said. "We'll never get across the road with it now. Leave everything in the orchard. I'll send a crew over to pick it up tonight around midnight. Come on, Boots. We'll go out the emergency exit and take off across the road."

"But—" Diane protested.

She was too late. Bruno pulled the lever and kicked open the door. The bus exploded with a loud alarm buzzer. Bruno grabbed a shocked Boots and the two shot across the road to their own campus, leaving chaos and confusion behind them.

"Who did that?" shrilled Miss Scrimmage.

Nobody answered.

"I tried to tell them," Diane whispered to Cathy, who was laughing too hard to reply.

"Who did that?" repeated Miss Scrimmage.

"It must be defective," called out Cathy finally. "It's a good thing someone didn't fall out on the way home."

"Quite right," fumed Miss Scrimmage. "I shall complain to the bus company."

* * *

"I'm glad to see we're all present and accounted for," said Bruno at the dinner table.

"Barely," muttered Wilbur.

"Some guy was after us at the dump," said Pete. "If it hadn't been for Sidney's quick thinking, we'd have got caught."

"Quick thinking, my eye!" retorted Wilbur. "It was clumsiness, as usual."

The boys broke into a confused babble of complaints about their experiences on the hunt, all directed at Bruno Walton.

"Most important," cried Bruno over the din, "did you guys get a lot of cans?"

"When you see Dormitory 3," said Larry, "you'll freak out! We've got them stacked four high and they take up the first nine doorways! I didn't think there were that many cans in the world!"

"Scrimmage's has a lot too," said Boots.

"We're all going over there to get them tonight," Bruno added.

"Count me out," chorused everybody.

"If we don't get them," responded Bruno cheerfully, "all that work we did last night will be for nothing."

Wilbur held his head. "What do we have to do?"

"Each of you recruit a few more guys," instructed Bruno. "We need lots of muscle. We'll all meet tonight in front of Dormitory 2."

"Is this mandatory?" asked Elmer in a small voice.

"Absolutely," said Bruno.

Elmer sighed. "I was afraid of that."

"When are we going to build this pyramid anyway?" asked Boots.

"Next Saturday," Bruno told them. "That's the day The Fish and most of the staff go to Toronto for the big Board meeting. I've already called the TV station in Chutney to come and witness it for us."

"We're going to be on TV?" gasped Pete.

"Publicity *and* the *Rankin Book of World Records*," said Bruno with great satisfaction.

A question of ownership

At midnight Cathy Burton and Diane Grant were at their window watching as about twenty-five Macdonald Hall students arrived at Miss Scrimmage's apple orchard. It took the boys only a few minutes to locate the treasure of pop cans the girls had hidden there for them. Then, carrying four big bags apiece, the boys began to move slowly and silently back towards Macdonald Hall.

In the lead, Bruno and Boots were just about to step onto the highway.

"*Halt!*"

The whole group stopped and wheeled about. Miss Scrimmage was running towards them, her arms waving wildly. She did not, Bruno was relieved to note, have her shotgun.

"*Run!*" he bellowed, and twenty-five yelling boys, each carrying huge clanking bundles, thundered across the highway with Miss Scrimmage in hot pursuit. In a matter of seconds, a stream of girls dressed in nightclothes swarmed after them.

"No!" howled Bruno, seeing his crew heading for Dormitory 3. "Don't lead her there!" He could not be heard over the general din. "No! Stop! Awwwww . . . " He ran after them.

Boys began to pour out of Dormitories 1 and 2, sleepy and bewildered.

"Stop, thieves!" screeched Miss Scrimmage, still running at the head of her army of shrieking girls.

The boys arrived at Dormitory 3, threw the door open and stampeded inside, dropping their bags and kicking the neatly stacked pop cans all over the hall. Sidney Rampulsky was the first to fall. He started a chain reaction, and soon all twenty-five boys were down on the floor, pop cans scattered all around them. More boys were pouring in through the doorway, all tripping and tumbling.

"What's going on?"

"Our pop cans!"

"Miss Scrimmage is coming! She's going to find our pop cans!"

"Don't be silly! What would she do with thirty-two thousand pop cans?"

"Ouch!"

Outside, a hysterical Miss Scrimmage was being restrained by several of her girls.

"Don't go in there, Miss Scrimmage," Diane Grant pleaded. "You won't like it!"

"Release me!" insisted Miss Scrimmage.

The girls' gym teacher, Miss Smedley, arrived on the scene. "Miss Scrimmage," she shrilled, "all the girls have left their rooms!"

"I can see that!" cried the Headmistress.

From room 200 in Dormitory 2, Coach Flynn's head appeared. "Shut up out there!" he bellowed. He took in the wild scene and exclaimed in horror, "What the heck is going on?"

"It's Al!" cried Cathy. "Hi, Al!"

"Are you all crazy?" shouted Flyn. "Get off our campus! Go back where you belong!"

"*Release me!*" shrilled Miss Scrimmage once more.

Bruno finally scrambled out the door of Dormitory 3.

"Walton!" yelled Flynn. "What are you doing out of bed?"

"There's one of them!" cried Miss Scrimmage. "Stop, thief!" She pulled herself loose, and arms waving, began to chase Bruno around the building. A crowd of her girls followed, screaming for her to come back. Boots darted after them.

Bruno gulped as he ran. Approaching on the dead run was a familiar figure in a red silk bathrobe and bedroom slippers. It was Mr. Sturgeon.

"Hello, sir," panted Bruno as they met.

The Headmaster thrust Bruno behind him, held up both hands and announced quietly and firmly, "Stop this *at once*!"

Boots ran up and joined Bruno behind Mr. Sturgeon.

"Now," cried Miss Scrimmage triumphantly, "proof at last! Your boys robbed our school!"

"Miss Scrimmage . . . " began Cathy uneasily.

The Headmistress pointed to Dormitory 3. "There is where they stashed the loot! Just have a look inside!"

"I believe I will," responded a grim-faced Mr. Sturgeon in a controlled voice. The crowd parted to let him through. He walked around the corner of the building to the front door and looked inside. His jaw dropped in amazement. About fifty of his students were inside, wallowing in a sea of shiny pop cans. The scene resembled a battle in a bad science-fiction movie.

Miss Scrimmage caught up to him. "You see? They stole my girls' souvenirs from—" She stopped in midsentence to stare at the spectacle.

Cathy nudged Diane. "Boy, oh boy," she whispered. "The soda pop is going to hit the fan now."

Mr. Sturgeon cleared his throat purposefully. "You boys come out of there at once."

"I'm trying, sir!" cried Sidney Rampulsky, hopelessly attempting to swim to the door.

Mr. Sturgeon turned to Miss Scrimmage. "As you can see," he said icily, "*nothing* has been stolen from your school. In the interests of peace and quiet, then, I think the best thing for you to do is to depart." His face turned momentarily red, indicating suppressed anger. "*At once,* if you please."

Miss Scrimmage gathered up her staff and students and began to march towards home.

Mr. Sturgeon turned to his boys. "You will all go to your beds immediately." The boys began to scatter, grateful to be out of the Headmaster's presence. "Walton, O'Neal, not you. I will see you in my office."

"But, sir," protested Bruno, "the Faculty Building is locked up for the night."

"I am entrusted with a key," replied Mr. Sturgeon, producing a key ring from his dressing gown pocket. "Come with me. We shall discuss this while it is still fresh in our minds."

Silently Bruno and Boots followed the Headmaster into the darkened Faculty Building. Mr. Sturgeon switched on the lights in his office and led the boys inside. Instinctively, they seated themselves on the bench.

Mr. Sturgeon closed the door and began pacing in front of them, his backless slippers flapping loudly. "Now," he said grimly, "I want an explanation. From the beginning. Everything. Omit nothing. A complete and concise summary of all the events leading up to the presence of that abomination in our dormitory!"

There was an awful silence.

"Come, come!" Mr. Sturgeon prodded. "You cannot possibly get into any more trouble than you are already in! I wish to know this instant why our dormitory is burgeoning with tin cans!"

"Well, sir," began Bruno. There seemed no way out of

it, and he was about to resort to the truth. "It's like this. We were—"

There was the sound of running feet in the hall outside. The door flew open and in burst Cathy Burton in a pink quilted dressing gown and matching fur slippers.

"Oh, sir," she panted, throwing herself at Mr. Sturgeon's feet, "I confess! The pop cans—they're mine!"

Mr. Sturgeon jumped back as if he had been burned. "You will remove yourself from the floor, young lady," he commanded sternly.

Cathy got up and sat down on the bench between Bruno and Boots.

Oh, no, thought Boots miserably. If she's trying to get away with the same stuff she pulls on Miss Scrimmage, The Fish'll cut all three of us to pieces!

"Cathy ... " murmured Bruno warningly.

"Silence!" thundered Mr. Sturgeon. He seated himself at his desk. "You are Miss Burton, I believe. Tell me, Miss Burton, how did you come into the possession of so many soft-drink cans?"

"I'm a collector, sir," Cathy explained. "I can never pass up a pop can. When I see them, I just have to have them." She detected the beginnings of a smile on Mr. Sturgeon's face and decided to elaborate. "I now have 41,683," she said proudly. "I'm one of the foremost collectors in the country."

"Congratulations," said Mr. Sturgeon dryly. "May I ask how this formidable collection came to reside in my dormitory?"

Cathy hung her head dramatically. "My collection got so big that it was clogging up my room. I needed more space. Of course, cans can't be stored outside. Rust and corrosion are the can collector's nightmares."

Mr. Sturgeon nodded understandingly. "Do go on," he prompted.

"The fact is, sir," Cathy confessed, "I talked Bruno and Melvin into letting me keep my collection in your empty dormitory. It was all my fault. I'm sorry." She gave him her most innocent, dark-eyed look.

Mr. Sturgeon indulged in a long coughing spell. Finally he asked, "Does Miss Scrimmage know about your celebrated collection?"

"Uh—no, sir," replied Cathy.

"Well," said the Headmaster, smiling broadly, "why don't we tell her?" He reached for the telephone.

"Hello, Miss Scrimmage," he said genially, much different from the man who had just ordered her off the campus. "I think I have straightened things out around here. There is a Miss Burton in my office at the moment ... No, she is here of her own free will. We have not kidnapped her ... I was hoping you would ask that. She is here to confess to ownership of the 41,683 soft drink containers which are currently in my dormitory. Isn't that right, Miss Burton?"

"Yes, sir," mumbled Cathy half-heartedly.

"Yes, they belong to her," Mr. Sturgeon continued in

great good humour, "and therefore to you . . . But it is the girl's *collection*, Miss Scrimmage, and quite an impressive one at that. It is not often that you see this sort of dedication in young people . . . Well, from what she tells me, you allotted no space at your school for this monumental project. It seems to me that you have sadly neglected the specialized interests of one of your young ladies. The poor girl is very upset. That is why I do not intend to punish my lads. Even though they did not consult me, I consider their housing Miss Burton's collection an extremely commendable act. However"—he was enjoying himself hugely—"now that you know about the existence of this wondrous collection, I'm sure that you will want to claim it for your school. So I expect it—all of it—to be out of my dormitory by noon tomorrow . . . Oh, no, no, don't disturb yourself at this hour, Miss Scrimmage. I shall escort Miss Burton home. Goodnight." By the time he had hung up, the smile had grown even broader.

"Off to bed, boys," he said to Bruno and Boots. "Come along, Miss Burton. I'll take you home."

* * *

"I could just choke!" exclaimed Bruno Walton as he and Boots walked down the hall of Dormitory 2. "When I think of all those cans! We had a world record in the palm of our hand, and it all turned to gazoobies!"

"We got away with it, though," Boots pointed out.

"Cathy saved our lives! Did you see the way she handled The Fish? I don't understand it. She told him the most ridiculous story and he fell for it like a jerk. *We* never could have gotten away with that."

"Yeah," agreed Bruno, "but if we'd admitted the cans were ours he couldn't have socked it to Miss Scrimmage. He loves getting the best of her."

"So long as we don't get expelled," Boots sighed.

"We don't have to get expelled," mourned Bruno. "No pop cans, no pyramid, no record, no publicity, no enrolment, no Macdonald Hall."

He opened the door to room 201 and switched on the light, startling Elmer who had, in the end, been exempted from pop-can duty. Elmer was on his knees tinkering by flashlight with a huge mechanical device which had materialized in the centre of the room in place of the chemistry lab. That had been pushed to a corner and had not been used since the incident with Coach Flynn. Flynn, who had been more than bewildered about losing a day somewhere, still had his cold.

"On the plus side," muttered Boots, "no Macdonald Hall, no Elmer Drimsdale."

"Where have you been?" asked Elmer anxiously. "What happened?"

"Miss Scrimmage again," moaned Bruno. "The pop cans are gone. End of pyramid. Zap." He threw himself onto his bed. "She caught us with Elmer; she caught us with Sidney; she was there when you lost your shoe; she darn near got us sneaking off her bus; and she got us tonight and ruined our pyramid! I don't know what I'm going to *do* with that woman!"

Boots pointed to the immense contraption towering over Elmer. "What on earth is *that*?"

"It's the new remote control device I'm working on," Elmer replied.

"What does it do?" asked Boots.

"It is an extremely inexpensive remote-control guidance system with a high-speed capability," explained Elmer.

"What's so great about that?" murmured Bruno, depressed and weary. "Everybody flies model airplanes."

"Not, I believe, at these speeds—nor for the price," replied Elmer. "If it's successful, it may be an extremely important discovery."

Bruno was suddenly interested. "Do you think it will get us lots of publicity?"

"I should think so," said Elmer cautiously.

"Okay," decided Bruno. "You work on that non-stop. We'll take care of your plants and ants and stuff. Meanwhile Boots and I will think of other records to set. I'm not going to let Macdonald Hall collapse because of Miss Scrimmage!"

"Couldn't we go to sleep now?" yawned Boots. "We haven't slept since Thursday!"

Bruno, fully dressed, was already asleep.

* * *

"Catherine, I'm shocked," said Miss Scrimmage. "Shocked and disappointed." The two were in Miss Scrimmage's sitting room having a late night discussion over warm milk. "Haven't I always been a fair Headmistress? You should have come to me when you needed someplace to keep your collection. I'm very hurt."

"I'm sorry, Miss Scrimmage," murmured Cathy. "I was afraid you'd think collecting pop cans was unladylike."

"Nonsense, dear," replied the Headmistress. "It's a lovely hobby. We can keep your collection in the empty storage room in the basement. It's dry and comfortable and always locked, so your cans will be perfectly safe there."

"Oh, thank you, Miss Scrimmage," said Cathy gratefully.

"Now, run along to bed, dear, and we'll say no more about the events of this night."

Congratulating herself on a successful evening, Cathy went to her room.

* * *

"William!" exclaimed Mrs. Sturgeon as her husband entered the kitchen where she was brewing tea. "What happened? You look ten years younger!"

"Mildred, you would have died!" chuckled the Headmaster. He told her about the riot and the pop cans in Dormitory 3. "And I had Walton and O'Neal dead to rights. They were just about to tell all when that awful Burton girl burst in. You won't believe this! She said the cans were hers and that she's a collector! Forty thousand of them! Mildred, that girl should be on the stage! You never saw such a performance!"

"Surely you told her that you didn't believe it," said Mrs. Sturgeon.

"I did nothing of the kind!" chortled her husband. "I called up Miss Scrimmage and lectured her about neglecting the interests of her students. Lord, I enjoyed it! I cannot recall enjoying anything so much!"

"What about the boys?" she asked. "That was a terrible disturbance. Are you going to punish them?"

"Punish them?" he laughed. "I should reward them for providing me with such a golden opportunity! Why, I gave Miss Scrimmage until noon to get that rubbish collection off my campus. And I intend to supervise the removal personally."

"But, William, you *know* the cans belong to our boys."

"Of course I know," he replied. "But now they belong to Miss Scrimmage—all forty thousand of them. And you missed it!"

"Sit down," she suggested. "A nice cup of tea will bring you down to earth."

"Actually, there's only one thing that disturbs me," remarked Mr. Sturgeon. "Two things, really." He frowned. "How did our boys amass forty thousand soft-drink containers? And more important, what in the world were they going to do with them?"

Euclid is Putrid

Bruno Walton crawled out of bed late on Sunday morning and went listlessly over to Elmer's video broadcast machine. He flicked the *On* button.

* * *

The head of Mighty Mouse disappeared from Sergeant Featherstone's TV set, to be replaced by the familiar fish.

Thanks to a certain somebody, the audio crackled, *Operation Popcan was a complete and total disaster with absolutely no redeeming features.*

A great feeling of elation surged through Featherstone. All the misery and discomfort had been worth it. He had foiled Operation Popcan!

The voice went on. *The Fish Patrol has decided that activities cannot go on unless this certain somebody is out of the way. Be warned. The Fish will have revenge!*

Featherstone was stunned. They were planning to dispose of him! He rushed into the bathroom to dictate his report.

* * *

"Bruno, why do you keep doing that?" asked Boots, who had also slept in that morning. "You know no one can hear it."

"It's an outlet for my frustrations," said Bruno. "Miss Scrimmage is driving me crazy."

"How are you going to get her out of the way?" asked Boots. "You can't murder her."

"Much as I'd like to," muttered Bruno. He wandered to the window and lifted the blind. "Will you look at that!"

A long line of girls stretched from Dormitory 3 all the way across the road to Miss Scrimmage's. At the door of the dormitory stood the Headmistress herself, supervising the removal of the pop cans and casting an occasional fuming look at Mr. Sturgeon who had established himself in a lawn chair and was watching the proceedings with great interest.

Boots came to the window. "There go our pop cans," he observed with mixed emotions.

Bruno nodded sadly. "But we're not dead yet. There are lots of ways to get publicity."

The door opened and Elmer Drimsdale climbed in over Boots's bed and made his way around the equipment to his newest device. "Good morning," he said. "I was just down the hall getting some things I need from Larry's radio. Since Sidney broke it anyway, Larry said I could have the parts."

"Great," said Bruno. "Get to work. But first, tell us

what you want us to do with your plants and stuff."

Elmer whipped out a sheaf of papers half an inch thick. "I've prepared a booklet outlining your duties," he said, handing the papers to Boots.

Bruno and Boots sat down to read their instructions as Elmer commenced tinkering on his remote-control machine.

Bruno looked up helplessly. "Elmer, how am I supposed to tell the difference between Aspidistra 7 and Boston Fern 3?"

"The fern has serrated leaves," explained Elmer, "while the aspidistra's leaves are green and white striped. Besides, the names and numbers are marked on the pots."

"Oh."

"I'll do the ants," offered Boots. "Ants are my specialty."

The three boys set out to complete their respective tasks.

* * *

Sergeant Harold P. Featherstone, Junior, watched and waited. It was after noon when the tall thin man with the long nose came out of room 14, got into his car and drove away. Silently Featherstone crept out of his room and stepped over to the next door. From his belt he produced a long, narrow object which he inserted carefully into the lock, moving it painstakingly. Five minutes passed. The click which his training had told him to expect was not forthcoming. He jiggled for another few minutes, reflecting that the entire population of Chutney had by then had enough time to spot him crouched before the door of room 14. Frustrated, he stood up and kicked the wall. There was a click and the door swung wide. Removing the lock-pick, he dashed inside and shut the door.

Room 14 was exactly like room 13, small and drab. The bed had not yet been made, and there was a towel lying on the floor. Some of the man's clothes were draped over a chair. The wastebasket held nothing but three apple cores and a plum pit. In the suitcase was more clothing and a book. Featherstone quivered with excitement. The book was a well-thumbed paperback entitled *Fish of the World*.

"A code book!" he exclaimed aloud. He had always believed that the Fish was sending coded messages to his underlings through the public television channels, and the existence of this book seemed to prove it.

He was about to examine it when the sound of a car outside caught his attention. He stuffed the book into his hip pocket and ran into the bathroom, where the window looked out on the bushy area back of the motel. He heard the key in the lock as he climbed up onto the sink and hoisted himself through the window, kicking the screen out as he went.

Splat! He fell flat on his face in mud. As he scrambled

up, he sank to his ankles in the slime. He could hear the man moving about in the room. He had to get out of there fast, and there was only one way. He pulled his feet out of the mud, leaving his shoes behind, and ran around the building to the safety of his own room.

In room 14, the tall man walked into his bathroom. The window was wide open, the screen gone. Hoisting himself up, he looked out the window. In the mud below lay his screen, and beside it, the full-length imprint of a body. Stuck in the mud was a pair of shoes.

The man frowned. His room had been searched.

* * *

At the dinner table that night the conversation was very pessimistic. The boys were tired and hostile. Macdonald Hall's austerity program was still in full force, and no-where was it more apparent than in the dining hall. The food did nothing to lighten the general mood.

"We need another plan," said Bruno.

"I haven't recovered yet from your last plan," snapped Wilbur. "I spent the night in the town dump rooting in garbage for nothing! It'll be a frosty Friday in July before I do anything else you tell me to!"

As if on cue, every boy within earshot began complaining.

"All that work for nothing!"

"My back was killing me!"

"It cost me two bucks bus fare!"

"I tell you there was a *guy* at the dump!"

"I almost got arrested for loitering!"

"Give me back that fig! It's mine!"

"I stepped on a cat in that alley!"

The general uproar was interrupted by Larry Wilson who came tearing into the dining hall as if he'd seen a ghost. "Bruno! Bruno, we've got trouble!"

"So what else is new?" said Wilbur sourly.

Larry ignored him and flopped into a chair. "I just heard at the office—on Saturday at two o'clock, when The Fish and most of the staff are in town for the Board meeting, a big real estate developer is coming out here to look at the land! He wants to buy Macdonald Hall and tear down everything to build apartments!"

"We can't let him do that!" exclaimed Pete. Other voices chorused his horrified reaction.

Bruno stood up. "Well, it's started, hasn't it? It's the beginning of the end." He looked reproachfully at Wilbur and the others. "And you guys have the nerve to complain! I wasn't trying to make you miserable! I was trying to save the Hall!" He pounded the table. "But it's not too late! We may have lost a battle, but the war's not over yet! Where would we be if Champlain had packed up and left because it got too cold here? Where would we be if Alexander Graham Bell had given up after the first wrong number?"

Bruno's face was red. All eyes were on him. "So we've had a little setback! Good men don't lie down and die because of one failure! If Macdonald Hall was worth the effort Friday night, it's worth the effort now! By being out all night, our guys beat the system, and we can beat this developer too! We're going to convince him that this is the *last* place anybody would want to build apartments! We'll chase him right back where he came from, and then some! We can defeat our enemies! We can overcome anything if we work at it! I know we can!"

Out of breath, he sat down amid thunderous applause from all present. Boys were standing on their chairs and chanting, "Can do! Can do!" In a far corner of the room, someone was leading a chorus of *We Shall Overcome*. Arms reached out to pat Bruno on the back.

Even Boots, who was not usually susceptible to Bruno's dramatics, was overcome. "That was great, Bruno!" he exclaimed fervently. "How are we going to get rid of the developer?"

"Don't undermine my moment of glory," whispered Bruno under cover of the general din. "I'll think of something later."

Boots opened his mouth to protest, but a group of boys grabbed Bruno, hoisted him to their shoulders and left the dining hall to carry him around the campus in a snake dance. A cheering crowd followed.

"He has no plan!" said Boots to thin air.

"I know," said Wilbur. "But he'll come up with something. And it'll land us all in the soup. But after a speech like that, what can we do?"

"Jump on the bandwagon like everybody else," grinned Boots.

* * *

Sergeant Featherstone pored over the book he had confiscated from room 14. He worked painstakingly, page by page, hoping to come upon some marking or any clue at all to the code in use. Suddenly he came to a page with a check mark on the top corner, directly above a drawing that looked exactly like the fish image appearing on the area TV screens. His heart began to pound with excitement, and he started to read:

The Pacific Salmon. In the North Pacific Ocean there is a family of salmon that belongs to the genus Oncorhynchus. The best known and most valuable of this species is the King salmon (Oncorhynchus Tshawytscha). This fish generally grows to four and a half feet in length. It is considered a great delicacy when served with chutney relish.

Featherstone almost dropped the book in his excitement. "Four and a half feet"—room 14! "Chutney relish" could only mean the township of Chutney and maybe ... the Chutney motel! *This* was the headquarters of the Fish organization. As for the "King salmon," that was obvious. The tall thin man with the long nose was no agent! He was the Fish himself!

Sergeant Featherstone breathed deeply. He was just one perilous step away from cracking the Fish conspiracy!

* * *

On Wednesday after classes, Bruno, Boots and Elmer were in their room trying to find space to do their homework.

"Bruno, how can you just sit there?" exclaimed Boots suddenly. "You got everybody all riled up and you don't even have a plan to get rid of that developer! What are we going to do?"

"I'll think of something," replied Bruno confidently.

They lapsed into studious silence for five minutes. Music from across the road wafted in through the open window.

"Pretty good," murmured Boots absently.

"What?" asked Bruno.

"Scrimmage's band. They're pretty good, don't you think?"

"Mmmm," nodded Bruno, his head buried in a math book.

"They're a little loud," commented Elmer. "After all, we do have to work here."

Bruno's head snapped to attention. "What? What? *What*? Say that again?"

"I said they're pretty good," said Boots.

"But a little loud," added Elmer.

Bruno's face took on a thoughtful expression. "But what if they were very bad? And *very* loud? Who would want to live across the street from that? Who would even want to *build* here?"

"Bruno, what are you saying?" asked Boots suspiciously.

With a joyful laugh Bruno tossed his math book into a pile of laundry. "I'm saying that by Saturday, with our help, of course, Miss Scrimmage's band is going to get a lot bigger, a lot louder, and a lot worse! That developer is going to head for the hills when he sees—and hears— what's across the road from his apartment building-to-be! Or not-to-be!"

"That is the question," muttered Boots. "And the answer is trouble. Bruno, we'll get expelled!"

"Nobody will see us," returned Bruno. "The Board meeting, remember?"

"What about Miss Scrimmage?" ventured Elmer timidly.

"Don't worry about her," scoffed Bruno. "By the time she figures out what's going on, the developer will be long gone."

"We'll have to set it up with the girls," said Boots. "Don't tell me we're going to Scrimmage's again tonight!"

"Are you kidding?" demanded Bruno. "That place is a death trap! Now, let's see, where can we get a telephone?"

"Are you crazy?" cried Boots. "Scrimmage wouldn't let Cathy talk to you!"

"Yes, she will," grinned Bruno. "Now, about that telephone . . . "

* * *

110

Larry Wilson, his messenger duties over for the day, tiptoed into the empty office of the English Department and shut the heavy oak door softly behind him. He opened the window, picked up the telephone from the desk and lowered it down to a pair of waiting hands outside in the bushes.

"Hurry!" he whispered.

Bruno dialled Miss Scrimmage's number.

"You'll never pull it off!" whispered Boots from beside him.

"Watch me." Bruno cleared his throat and in his very deepest voice said, "Good afternoon. This is Mr. Burton. I would like to speak with my daughter Catherine, please. It's very important." There was a long pause, then, "No, it's not Dad, Cathy, it's me—Bruno. Now listen carefully. We need your help . . . "

Briefly he explained the situation with the land developer. "We don't want him killed, you understand—just scared off. All you have to do is get the girls out on the lawn for band practice on Saturday at 1:45. Leave plenty of room, and don't be surprised if your band gets a lot bigger . . . No, don't worry about being good. Just be loud." He laughed. "Yes, I'll give your love to Mom, John and Susie. See you Saturday. 'Bye."

He passed the phone back through the window, whispering his thanks. Then he and Boots scampered off towards Dormitory 2.

* * *

"Eat your breakfast, dear. You don't want to be late for your Board meeting," said Mrs. Sturgeon early Saturday morning.

"I'm not very hungry," confessed the Headmaster glumly. "I don't like the idea of being in town while some real estate developer decides the fate of my school."

"I don't blame you," she agreed. "It was pretty shabby of them to make the appointment for today."

"It was not only shabby, it was probably deliberate. The Chairman doesn't want me here in case I might say something discouraging to the man." He chuckled without mirth. "I should invite Miss Scrimmage to come over and meet her prospective new neighbour. If that doesn't put him off, nothing will."

"Oh, William!" she exclaimed. "I can't believe this is happening to Macdonald Hall!"

He sighed. "I'm afraid we must face it, Mildred. Our days here are numbered. Would you please hand me my briefcase? I'd best be off."

* * *

Saturday lunch was just drawing to a close in Miss Scrimmage's pink and silver dining room when Cathy Burton got to her feet and tapped a spoon against her water glass for attention.

"All right, girls," she announced. "We're having a special kind of band practice today. I want the whole school

112

on the front lawn in fifteen minutes. Everyone should bring an instrument. That includes kazoos, harmonicas, whistles and combs with tissue paper."

"I don't have an instrument," called out one girl. Several other voices echoed the complaint.

"Take along your spoons and get a garbage can lid to bang on," Cathy replied. "We need percussion."

"What's it all about?" asked someone.

"Macdonald Hall is coming over," Cathy grinned. "We're going to update the big band sound."

The girls scattered, always ready for action.

In fifteen minutes the lawn in front of Miss Scrimmage's Finishing School for Young Ladies was teeming with young people. Most of them had makeshift instruments ranging from cigar box banjos to jars of stones to shake. There were also a number of genuine instruments, from jaw-harps to tubas. Cathy had brought out a microphone extension to Miss Scrimmage's P.A. system, for maximum volume.

"Hot gazoobies, we're going to blast that developer away!" exclaimed Bruno with great glee.

"We're certainly going to try," Cathy agreed. "Let's start!"

"No, no, no," begged Boots, tuning his guitar. "Let's wait till the developer gets here. If we start too soon, Miss Scrimmage will catch us."

"Oh, no," said Cathy. "She's not here. She went out to the beauty parlour for a check-up."

Bruno turned to Elmer Drimsdale. "Hey, Elm, where's your instrument?"

"Well," began Elmer, "I thought I'd just listen and—"

"What do you mean 'just listen'?" Cathy shrieked. "This is a combined effort! *Everybody* takes part!" She stuffed the microphone into his hands. "*You* are the vocalist!"

"I don't sing," protested Elmer weakly.

"Learn," chorused Cathy and Bruno.

"Here comes a truck!" shouted one of the boys.

"This is it!" screamed Cathy. "And-a-one, and-a-two, and-a-one-two-*three*!"

The band exploded into a riot of noise. Trumpets blared, garbage cans clanged, clarinets squeaked and bassoons groaned. Since no one had settled on a selection to play, every instrument was playing something different, and every tin plate and pot was banging a different rhythm. The effect was appalling.

Cathy kicked Elmer in the shins. "You're not singing!"

Elmer grasped the microphone, shut his eyes tightly and began to shout the only thing that came to his mind —scientific facts. "The area of a circle equals *pi* times the square of the radius!" he howled.

Bruno, who had been blowing foghorn noises through a vacuum cleaner hose, broke into hysterical laughter.

"A floating object displaces its own weight in liquid!" shouted Elmer, really getting into the spirit of his lyrics. "Congruent angles have congruent complements. The kangaroo is a marsupial! Isn't science wonderful? Oh, yes! Yes!"

The tremendous din went on as the truck pulled up and parked across the road. On the side in red block capitals was written CHUT-TV.

Bruno's laughter faded. "Oh, no!" he shouted at Boots. "I forgot to call them off!"

Two men got out of the truck, holding their ears and scanning the Macdonald Hall campus. Seeing no one there, they crossed the road towards the huge orchestra.

Cathy and Bruno held their hands up for silence and the noise petered out.

One of the men spoke. "Do any of you kids know where the world's largest tin-can pyramid is? We're here to film it and witness it for the *Rankin Book of World Records*."

"Never heard of it," said Bruno quickly.

"Oh, a hoax, eh? Any of you know this guy Walton who phoned us?"

"Never heard of him either," said Bruno.

"You know, Jack," said the second man, "Tupper expects us to come back with a story. Why don't we do something on these kids?" He went for his equipment.

"Good idea," said Jack. He turned to the band. "What do you kids call yourselves?"

Cathy stepped forward. "We are Elmer Dynamicdale and the Original Round-Robin Happy-Go-Lucky Heel-Clicking Foot-Stomping Beat-Swinging Scrim-Band," she said evenly. "Would you like me to repeat that?"

"If you think you can. How about doing a number? Get this Dynamicdale guy up front."

Bruno pushed Elmer and his microphone out in front of the camera.

"Okay," called the cameraman, "introduce yourselves and let 'er rip."

Cathy leaned towards the microphone clutched in Elmer's hands. "Hi, fans!" she shouted. "He's Elmer Dynamicdale, and we're the Original Round-Robin Happy-Go-Lucky Heel-Clicking Foot-Stomping Beat-Swinging Scrim-Band with the music of the future, our own invention, Science Rock! Here's Elmer with our biggest hit, *Euclid is Putrid*!"

Bruno began waving his arms and the band started again with even more enthusiasm and noise than before.

Cathy kicked Elmer, which seemed the only way to get him started.

"Geometry!" bawled Elmer. "The square on the hypotenuse of a right-angled triangle is equal to the sum of the squares of the other two sides! Another wonderful geometric fact! And over three hundred ways to prove it! The median to the base of an isosceles triangle is the perpendicular bisector of the base! And the triangle doesn't even have to be isosceles for the angle bisectors to be concurrent!"

"Wow, Jack, what do you think of them?" asked the cameraman, shouting over the racket.

"Those lead singers are getting weirder every day!" Jack shouted back. "Zoom in on Dynamicdale! Look at the faces he's making! This'll get a good laugh on the six o'clock news!"

"When a transversal crosses parallel lines, co-interior angles are supplementary!" Elmer sang out. "Similar triangles have proportional sides! Wow!" Now he was so excited that he was strutting around in front of the band, waving his microphone wildly. "Congruent figures have equal areas!"

"Okay, okay!" shouted the cameraman. "We've got enough! You can stop now! Please stop!"

Nobody heard. The din had completely drowned him out.

"The diagonals of a rhombus are perpendicular!" howled Elmer.

The two TV men ran for their truck, loaded their equipment and drove away in haste. The noise began to die out.

"Keep playing!" bellowed Bruno. "There's a car coming! It must be the developer!"

The racket swelled again.

A long, midnight-blue limousine pulled up and parked at the mouth of the driveway to Macdonald Hall. A uniformed chauffeur jumped out and opened the rear door. Out stepped the developer, a short, squat man in a grey business suit. He held his ears and winced. Encouraged, the band played louder.

"The sine of any angle equals the cosine of its complement!" yowled Elmer, who was now well into trigonometry.

Both men approached, waving their arms in a plea for silence. The din faded.

"Hello, sir," said Bruno with a wide, toothy grin. "How may we help you?"

"You can tell me what you're doing here," said the short, fat man curtly.

"We're having our band practice, sir," explained Cathy. "Practice makes perfect. That's what our music teacher says."

The developer looked sick. "Do you do this often?"

"Three times a day," said Bruno cheerfully.

"Usually at night," Cathy added.

"We're usually louder," added Bruno, "but a lot of the kids are away for the day."

"What's more, we are always scientifically accurate," said Elmer Drimsdale.

"Listen to how good we are!" yelled Cathy. "One, two, three—" The band erupted once more, with Elmer shouting something about prehistoric reptiles. This time he had not even required kicking.

Down the highway rolled Miss Scrimmage's black pick-up truck, with the Headmistress at the wheel.

"Tyrannosaurus Rex stood twenty feet high!" howled Elmer as the garbage cans clanged, the trombones moaned and the flutes tweetled.

From the driver's seat, Miss Scrimmage gaped in horror at the sight of her teeming front lawn. She was leaning across the seat, hanging her head out the window and screaming wildly, but no sound could be heard over the tremendous noise of the orchestra.

Crash! Miss Scrimmage's pick-up veered aimlessly across the highway and plowed into the limousine parked on the soft shoulder. The music died abruptly.

"Oh, no!" moaned Boots in the silence.

"Are you crazy, lady?" bellowed the developer. The front of his limousine was mangled beyond recognition. The radiator was spewing water, the hood was crumpled like an accordian, and the windshield was smashed.

Dropping their instruments, Miss Scrimmage's girls rushed to her rescue.

"Yes, yes, girls, I'm perfectly all right," the Headmistress assured them. "It was only a little accident."

"A little accident!" screamed the developer. "That was an eighteen thousand dollar car!"

"Now, now," shrilled Miss Scrimmage. "None of the children were hurt, and that's the main thing." She smiled at her girls and glared at the boys from Macdonald Hall. "Shoo! Get away! Leave my girls alone!"

That was all the encouragement the boys needed. They picked up their instruments and stampeded across the road towards home.

* * *

So it was that when Mr. Sturgeon returned to Macdonald Hall after his Board meeting he found a large tow-truck trying to separate the remains of a limousine from Miss Scrimmage's pick-up truck.

Bruno Walton was on the scene to offer an explanation.

"I think the man in that limo was coming to Macdonald Hall, sir. Miss Scrimmage came barrelling down the road on the wrong side. Boy, did she clobber him! The guy was so mad that he called a taxi and went back to Toronto. He says he's going to sue Miss Scrimmage blue!"

The Headmaster was facing away from him, but Bruno could see that he was smiling.

Bruno was smiling too. He had finally found a good use for Miss Scrimmage.

But will it fly?

"Miss Scrimmage," said Mr. Sturgeon into the telephone on Sunday morning, "I do not follow your line of reasoning. How can it possibly be the fault of Macdonald Hall that your automobile insurance rates are going up? ... And I also strongly doubt that my boys were over on your lawn scaring your girls with loud noise. It has been my experience that nothing scares your girls ... Miss Scrimmage, right beside the accelerator is another pedal. It activates the braking mechanism. Its function is to stop your vehicle's forward movement, thus avoiding an incident such as occurred yesterday. I would venture to say that any of my boys, without a lesson or a licence, could figure that out ... I am not 'bugging' you, Miss Scrimmage. *You* telephoned *me*. Good day."

"William," said his wife thoughtfully, "the boys *were* over there yesterday. I told you they were getting the two school bands together. They were even on the early news last night."

"Yes," said Mr. Sturgeon with a crooked smile. "That's the last time I leave Mr. Fudge in charge of the campus. He was probably taking a nap, and they say nothing wakes him up. The point is, however, that even though our boys had no business being over at Scrimmage's they were not at the wheel of the truck when it drove into that limousine. Miss Scrimmage was."

"That car belonged to the land developer, didn't it? The one who was coming here to look at Macdonald Hall?"

"It did. Miss Scrimmage seems to have adequately deterred him." Mr. Sturgeon switched on the television set. "The band was on the news, you say? Maybe it will be on again this morning. It's almost time for the ten o'clock report."

They watched a cartoon for a few minutes, and then the local newscaster came on the air. He smiled, opened his mouth to speak, and vanished. Once again the fish image monopolized the screen. The audio crackled with static, then a voice said, *A certain someone proved to be an asset rather than a liability yesterday. We of the Fish Patrol extend our thanks.* There was a wicked laugh. *We will crush all who oppose us. Beware the Fish!*

The newscaster reappeared.

"Mildred," said Mr. Sturgeon, perplexed, "why does that comment ring a bell? Why do I have the feeling that I should know that voice?"

"Oh, you're just tired and overwrought, dear," soothed his wife. "Have another cup of coffee."

* * *

Sergeant Featherstone stared at the television set in horror as the fish faded away. The 'certain someone,' who was obviously Featherstone himself, had been of assistance to the Fish's operation! But how? How could he have done these fiends a favour? Could it be that he, an officer of the law, had unwittingly become a tool in the hands of the forces of evil?

But he had done nothing in the past few days beyond acquiring and studying the Fish's code book. They were bluffing. They had to be. He was getting close. They had found that he could not be scared off by threats of violence, and now they were trying to make him believe that the code book was worthless.

Oh, yes, he was getting very close.

* * *

"Bruno, what are you moping about?" asked Boots. "We've been on television, haven't we?"

"Yeah," said Bruno savagely. "In front of Scrimmage's school as the Scrim-Band! That kind of publicity does nothing for Macdonald Hall!"

"Well, we got rid of the developer," pointed out Boots optimistically.

"If he's really dead set on building those apartments," retorted Bruno, "he'll be back. He won't let Miss Scrimmage stop him."

"It's ready," announced Elmer.

"Not now, Elm," said Bruno, still talking to Boots. "And as for the band practices," he went on, "I guess we were pretty stupid to think that a little noise would drive a guy away from a multi-million-dollar business deal."

"It's ready," repeated Elmer.

"What's ready?" asked Bruno impatiently.

"My remote control device," said Elmer. "It's ready for testing."

"Well, why didn't you say so?" cried Bruno, jumping to his feet. "How do we go about testing it?"

"We simply take it outdoors and fly it," said Elmer.

"Great," exclaimed Bruno. "We'll do it right now. Where's the best place?"

"Actually, the only place to test the mechanism properly would be in an area where there are trees. This would enable me to test the manoeuvrability, and more important, to see how my signals travel when there are solid obstacles about."

"What about the woods right in back?" suggested Boots.

Elmer shook his head. "No good. The trees are much too close together. There would be a crash."

"Scrimmage's apple orchard," decided Bruno. "It's perfect."

"Yes, it would be ideal," Elmer agreed. "However, I strongly doubt that Mr. Sturgeon or Miss Scrimmage would grant permission, relations being rather strained lately between our two respective schools."

"Yes," agreed Bruno, "but they couldn't object if they didn't know about it."

"No," said Boots simply, "we're not going there again."

"Don't be ridiculous!" scoffed Bruno. "The old girl guards her young ladies, not her apples. We're going tonight."

"Uh," protested Elmer uneasily, "I'm not sure I want to—"

"What a pair of chickens!" interrupted Bruno. "The matter is settled." To emphasize his point, he switched on Elmer's video machine.

* * *

Greetings once more from the Fish Patrol, crackled the now-familiar voice from Featherstone's television set. *We announce that Operation Flying Fish will commence tonight at midnight. You never know when the Fish may descend on you. Beware the Fish*!

"But where?" exclaimed Featherstone in frustration as the fish image disappeared from the screen. He knew only one thing. It was up to him to foil Operation Flying Fish as he had Operation Popcan. If only he knew where to begin.

* * *

"That is so annoying!" exclaimed Mrs. Sturgeon, switching off the TV. "They just can't seem to put a stop to it!"

"Mildred," said the Headmaster, "I know that voice. I'm sure I do. I just can't place it."

"Well, whoever it is," she said, "I hope they catch him and punish him severely. I'm sick of this."

Mr. Sturgeon frowned. "I'm positive I know that voice . . ."

* * *

At half-past eleven that night Sergeant Featherstone left his motel room and got into his car, intent on searching for Operation Flying Fish.

He wasn't going to the Chutney town dump, he decided. That was the last place they'd use as a base of operations after he'd been there to spoil Operation Popcan for them. And so, for lack of inspiration, he turned off Main Street in the opposite direction.

The door of room 14 opened and the cadaverous man hurried out and got into his car. The tires squealed as he started out in pursuit of Featherstone.

* * *

The midnight solitude of Miss Scrimmage's apple orchard was disturbed as three shadowy figures, laden with parcels, eased themselves over the wire fence and crept into the cover of the trees.

"Here's a good spot," said Bruno, dropping his burden.

Elmer, too frightened to speak, nodded.

Boots was also nervous. "Any sign of Miss Scrimmage? Or her shotgun?"

Bruno did not reply. "Okay, Elmer, set it up."

Obediently Elmer got to work. In fifteen minutes he had assembled a large console with operating buttons and a tall antenna. In his hands he held a metal sphere studded with Christmas tree lights.

"You're going to fly *that*?" asked Bruno. "That's not an airplane."

Elmer flicked a switch on the console to turn on the green and red bulbs. "This will fly," he replied with great satisfaction.

"Well?" said Bruno impatiently. "Let's see it."

"Do you have to have it lit up like that?" asked Boots. "We don't want old Scrimmage over here, you know!"

Elmer placed the ball inside a black tube attached to the console. "I must see it if I'm going to guide it," he explained patiently. "And now the test."

"Wait!" said Bruno suddenly, pulling the ball out of the tube. "It's bad luck to launch a ship without a name." With a marking pen he carefully printed *M.H. Flying Fish* on a clear patch of the metal.

"M.H.?" questioned Boots.

"Macdonald Hall, of course," said Bruno. He returned the little craft to the tube. "And now the test," he mimicked.

Elmer flicked a switch and turned a dial. There was a clunk, and the M.H. Flying Fish rocketed out of the tube and hovered among the branches of the trees, humming as it awaited instructions.

"Hot gazoobies!" cheered Bruno as he and Boots stared at the ball, which illuminated the portion of the orchard where they stood.

Skillfully Elmer manipulated the controls, putting his craft through a series of manoeuvres in, around and over the trees.

Suddenly there was a rustling in the darkness behind them and a voice called, "Halt!"

The three boys wheeled in horror.

Cathy Burton appeared from behind a tree. "Just kidding," she grinned. She glanced behind her. "Come on out, Diane. I told you it had to be them."

Diane appeared at her side. "What are you guys doing? What is that thing?"

"It's our ship," replied Bruno. "Elmer'll explain it to you."

Elmer shook his head violently, unable to speak in the presence of the girls.

"Oh, it's Elmer!" said Cathy. She strode over to the console. "Hey, decent! What does this thing do?" She grasped one of the dials and twisted it as far as it would go.

"No!" cried Elmer.

The M.H. Flying Fish shot up and away into the sky. Elmer frantically hit buttons, but to no avail. The hum of the motor was gone. The distant lights could no longer be seen.

"Our ship!" cried Bruno. "Bring it back!"

"I can't," said Elmer sadly. "It's out of range."

"Oops," said Cathy. "Sorry."

"Cath-y!" moaned Bruno in anguish. "That was going to make us famous, and you lost it!"

"Sorry," repeated Cathy. "Maybe you can build another one." She smiled brightly. "Anybody want something to eat?"

"I want to go home," groaned Elmer miserably.

"Yeah," muttered Boots. "Let's get out of here."

"Are you very mad?" asked Cathy penitently.

Bruno shrugged. "It's gone. I guess killing you won't change that."

The three boys picked up their equipment.

"Intruders halt!" shrieked a voice in the distance.

"A perfect ending to a perfect evening!" moaned Boots.

"Here she comes again," agreed Cathy. "You guys get going."

"What about you?" asked Bruno.

"Oh, don't worry about us," said Cathy. "If she catches us, we'll just tell her you've been terrorizing us again."

Carrying their equipment, the three boys vaulted the fence and ran off into the night.

* * *

Featherstone cruised aimlessly, alert for anything unusual that might be part of Operation Flying Fish. All was quiet. The farmhouses were dark, the fields deserted.

Suddenly he heard a strange distant humming noise. He rolled down the window to listen. Yes, it was definitely a hum, and it was growing louder. He stopped the car and stuck his head out the window.

"What the heck?" he gasped.

In the sky, approaching rapidly from the south, was a brightly lit UFO.

There was a sudden screeching of brakes, and Featherstone turned just in time to see another car skid out and around in front of him, missing him by a hair. He gaped in horror. It was the man from room 14, the Fish! It was a trap! He had been lured out here onto a lonely road . . .

The UFO was almost upon him now, but the Fish was blocking the highway. Blindly Featherstone pushed the accelerator to the floor. The small car shot off the road and smashed through an old wooden fence, coming to rest in the middle of a large pigpen. Frightened, squealing pigs stampeded through the hole in the fence, disappearing into the night.

Featherstone kicked madly at the gas pedal. The tires spun in the mud, but the car would not move. Desperately he looked around. He could see the UFO clearly now as it bore down on him from the sky, its red and green lights outlining a round body.

Plop! The object landed in the mud of the pigpen not

a foot from the car.

"Take cover!" shouted Featherstone to himself. Frantically he kicked the door open and threw himself out of the car to land face-down in the slop trough. He lay there tensely, waiting for an explosion. Nothing happened.

Cautiously he stole a look at the device. The green and red lights were flickering out, and the hum was dying. Slowly he picked himself up out of the trough and stood, dripping slops, staring down at the ball lying in the mud. The hum was gone now, the lights out. The sole remaining pig approached the now-dead UFO and rooted at it with his snout. Then, finding it of little interest, he too trotted out through the hole Featherstone's car had made in the fence.

Covered in mud and pig slops, Featherstone tried to evaluate the situation he found himself in. Once again he could remember no precedent in the RCMP training manual. He glanced back at the road. The man from room 14 had left the scene. The round object, whatever it was, seemed to present no immediate danger. The first order of business, then, must be to extricate himself from the muck of the pigpen and get the UFO back to his motel room for examination. Featherstone wrinkled his nose ruefully—and a shower wouldn't hurt.

He glanced at his car. The mud was over the hubcaps. It was a job for a tow-truck, possibly even a wrecker. From his pocket he produced an identification card, and with his index finger, wiped the mud from its face. He placed it under the windshield wiper for the benefit of the farmer, who was in for a shock. Then he tucked the surprisingly light UFO under his arm and began the long walk to Chutney, leaving a trail of mud and slime behind him.

*   *   *

"Miss Scrimmage," demanded Mr. Sturgeon into the telephone, "do you realize that it is almost two in the morning? . . . My boys were there doing *what*? . . . Bombs? Oh, yes, atomic bombs, no doubt . . . Oh, just ordinary bombs. Really, Miss Scrimmage, you must attempt to control your imagination. My boys do not have access to bombs . . . That's right, especially not flying bombs with red and green lights . . . Yes, well, Miss Scrimmage, sometimes our eyes deceive us. We've all been under considerable stress lately. Goodnight."

He turned to his wife. "Mildred, according to Miss Scrimmage, our boys laid down an artillery barrage on their campus tonight."

"That's nice," murmured Mrs. Sturgeon sleepily. "Go back to sleep, dear."

In the name of the law

"That Cathy!" muttered Bruno at the lunch table the following day. "I'd like to string her up by her ears!"

"It was just an accident, Bruno," argued Boots protectively. "She didn't mean it."

"It was also a flaw in my reasoning," admitted Elmer. "Because of the tremendous speed of the craft, I should have expanded the range of the controls." He sighed. "It was out of range in less than three seconds."

"Still," snapped Bruno, "that dippy girl—"

He was interrupted by a commotion at the entrance to the dining hall. The three boys ran to the centre of the disturbance. There, surrounded by a crowd of laughing students, marched a large pig. The animal was examining his new surroundings and glaring at the boys reproachfully as if they were trespassing on his territory.

"Hot gazoobies!" cried Bruno in delight. "We haven't had a guest for lunch since I don't know when!"

"This is our first pig," added Boots.

"Except for Wilbur!" shouted someone.

"Shut up!"

"Tell him to go away! There's not enough food here for us, let alone him!"

"Maybe he likes spinach!"

"Where did he come from?"

"I don't know. Hey! He's eating my lunch!"

"Just like Wilbur!"

"I said shut up!"

"Do you think we can keep him?"

"Keep whom?" asked a quiet voice from the doorway. A hush fell as Mr. Sturgeon entered the dining hall. His steely grey eyes surveyed the students and finally came to rest on the pig, whose head was now buried deep in one of the garbage cans. "May I ask how that creature came to be here?"

"He just arrived, sir," offered Bruno.

"I see," said the Headmaster. "By any chance, did anyone here assist his arrival?"

Nobody answered.

The silence was interrupted by the grinding of a truck motor outside. Mr. Sturgeon glanced outdoors to see a truckload of pigs pull up in front of the flagpole. "You will all remain here," he ordered, "and restrain the movements of that animal. I believe we shall be rid of him in a moment." He went out and motioned to the farmer to drive his truck up to the dining hall.

"Afternoon," said the farmer. "You folks got any of

my pigs here?"

Mr. Sturgeon smiled. "We do indeed."

"Darndest thing I ever saw," said the farmer, getting out of his truck. "Woke up this morning and found a car sitting in my pigpen. Big hole in the fence and all the pigs gone. Later some young fellow comes down with a tow-truck. They haul the car out of the pen and this guy gives me some money for the damages. Claims he was forced off the road by a flying bomb with red and green lights. Did you ever hear a story like that?"

Mr. Sturgeon choked. "A flying bomb with red and green lights," he repeated oddly. "There—seems to be a lot of that going around."

"First I heard of it," remarked the farmer. "Hope my pig didn't do any damage."

"No, indeed," replied Mr. Sturgeon. "He's just in here, and you're quite welcome to him."

With the help of the boys of Macdonald Hall, the farmer loaded his pig onto the truck with the others and drove off.

Mr. Sturgeon stood watching, scratching his head in utter confusion.

* * *

Featherstone sat on his bed turning the UFO over and over in his hands and observing it through a large magnifying glass. There was no doubt that it was some kind of device used by the notorious Fish, for written on the body of it in bold letters were the words *M.H. Flying Fish*.

Although puzzled, Sergeant Featherstone was exhilarated. He had once more ruined the Fish's operation. Unfortunately he had also ruined his car, his clothing and his left ankle, which hurt abominably. The war against terrorism obviously had its fortunes, good and bad.

M.H. Flying Fish. He puzzled over the letters M.H. Code, obviously. Well, his best bet was to hang around the room and hope for a fish broadcast on TV. Maybe that would add another clue.

* * *

"Mildred, am I going crazy?" asked Mr. Sturgeon over the dinner table.

"Why, William, what an extraordinary question! Of course not! What makes you ask such a thing?"

The Headmaster shook his head. "I'm not certain," he replied. "I've got a phantom voice talking at me from the television set, and now Miss Scrimmage's absurd story about red and green flying bombs seems to come from something other than her fevered imagination. That pig farmer knows someone who saw the same thing." Violently he speared a piece of cauliflower. "I'd like to know what's going on around here!"

"There's nothing going on around here, dear," his wife soothed.

"Well, then," he sighed, "I guess I *am* going crazy."

"Now, William . . ."

* * *

"It's hard to do homework," exploded Bruno Walton angrily, "when tomorrow you may not have a classroom or a teacher to hand it in to!"

"Meanwhile, the school is still here," soothed Boots, "and Elmer says he'll build another aircraft."

"Sure he will," said Bruno unhappily. "But right now he's on an overnight field trip with that enriched science group of his. That's twenty-four hours lost—twenty-four hours closer to having the Hall bought and paid for by some dippy developer. I just can't concentrate on math when the whole world is coming to an end!"

"Go talk to your fish," suggested Boots sarcastically. "Maybe you'll feel better."

"Good idea. I think I need it." Bruno got up and made his way over to Elmer's video machine.

* * *

This is the Fish Patrol in 201, came the voice. *Our Flying Fish flew away. In fact, things are so rotten around here that even the pigs won't stay. But we'll fight to the bitter end! Beware the Fish!*

Mr. Sturgeon grasped the arms of his chair and sat bolt upright. "201," he repeated. "2 – 0 – 1! *Walton!*"

"Pardon me, dear?" questioned his wife.

The Headmaster rose and began to pace nervously. "It

has to be! That's *his* voice! The flying fish! The pigs won't stay! Walton!"

"William, you're not making sense!" she protested.

He did not even hear her.

"But how?" he asked aloud. An awful picture began forming in his mind, a picture of Bruno Walton doing all the things Miss Scrimmage had accused the school of. She had raved about bombs, beatings, terrorist activities! What if she were right?

But that was ridiculous! How could she be right? Those pop cans—what did they have to do with it? What was Walton up to? Where would he get a flying bomb? What was the purpose of the big orchestra? Could he possibly be spending all that time at Scrimmage's, as much time as the regular complaints from the Headmistress indicated? And where did *they* fit in, anyway? What about Miss Scrimmage's tale of a member of his staff running about in his underwear? That *couldn't* have happened! What was this fish patrol and all the talk about fighting to the bitter end? It all had no meaning. And, most perplexing of all, how could Walton insert himself on television that way, seemingly at will? The entire thing was absolutely impossible! Jumping to hysterical conclusions was Miss Scrimmage's province. It wasn't for the staid, sensible Headmaster of Macdonald Hall. And yet . . .

Before his wife's astonished eyes, he rushed to the telephone and dialled a number.

"Hello, Flynn? Sturgeon here. I want you to send Bruno Walton over here immediately . . . No, to my home . . . At once, please . . . Thank you."

*   *   *

"Have I done anything lately?" asked Bruno after Flynn had delivered the Headmaster's message.

"What kind of a question is that?" demanded Boots nervously. "We've all done quite a lot lately!"

"No, I mean what have I done that The Fish would know about?" insisted Bruno, unperturbed.

"I've got a feeling that The Fish always knows what we're doing, every minute of every day," mourned Boots. "Bruno, what if he knows what's been going on?"

"Don't be an idiot," said Bruno. "How could he know? I see I'm not going to get any sense out of you, so I guess I'll have to go over there and ask The Fish himself."

"Good luck," murmured Boots, truly concerned.

Puzzled, Bruno jogged across the campus. He had never been ordered to the Headmaster's home before. What was so urgent that it couldn't wait for normal office hours? Oh well, he thought, employing one of his staunchest philosophies: never worry about what you can't avoid, there's only one way to find out. He approached the Headmaster's door and rang the bell.

Mr. Sturgeon opened the door and fixed his visitor with the coldest of fishy stares.

"You sent for me, sir?"

"I did," replied the Headmaster grimly. He looked into Bruno's innocent, questioning eyes and was struck dumb. Even before the boy's arrival, the Headmaster had not been sure of what he was going to say. Now he was even more uncertain. The whole thing seemed so ridiculous. How could he make such wild accusations to one of his students?

"Uh—sit down, Walton," he said, ushering Bruno into the living room. His wife had retreated upstairs. He paused, desperately trying to think how to phrase what he wanted to say.

"Yes, sir?" Bruno prompted.

"Lately," the Headmaster began slowly, "a lot of peculiar things have been happening. For instance, Miss Scrimmage's school has allegedly been suffering some extraordinary kinds of harassment, ranging from flying bombs to constant terrorism. Also, someone has been interfering with local television broadcasting. This whole part of the county has been complaining of seeing a large fish and hearing a voice speaking of a fish patrol."

Bruno turned a sickly shade of grey. His mouth moved, but no sound emerged.

"In a broadcast this evening," the Headmaster went on, "reference was made to some things which might pertain to Macdonald Hall." His voice took on a firm, commanding tone. "I have no proof, of course, and therefore I am not making any accusations. However, my main message is this: tomorrow morning, classes will be delayed. At nine o'clock sharp there will be a complete and thorough dormitory inspection of every room, made by me personally. I had better find everything in perfect order."

"Yes, sir," Bruno barely whispered.

"That will be all," said Mr. Sturgeon, standing up. "You are dismissed."

Bruno left the Headmaster's residence and dashed across the campus like an olympic sprinter. By the time he reached room 201 in Dormitory 2 he was breathless and even paler than before.

"Bruno, what's wrong? What happened?" cried Boots anxiously.

"I'm going to kill Elmer Drimsdale!" panted Bruno, rushing over to the video machine and ripping out wires at random. "Every time I've used this miserable tin-plated piece of garbage I've been on television! That dumb salmon poster and every word I've said! The Fish heard it all! All my fish jokes! *Everything*!"

Boots collapsed onto his bed. "Oh, no!"

"Oh, yes!" cried Bruno. "This thing has been telecasting to the whole area! Wait till I get my hands on Elmer!"

"The Fish knows!" moaned Boots.

"The Fish suspects," corrected Bruno, calming down. "Tomorrow morning there's going to be a big dorm inspection. And by the time that inspection rolls around, this video machine and all the other junk in this room are going to be gone!"

"Everything?" asked Boots.

"Everything," said Bruno grimly. "Miss Scrimmage has been complaining about all the stuff we've done. If The Fish makes the connection between her complaints and Elmer's gear, there'll be hot gazoobies all over the place! We have to get rid of everything, even the stuff we've had nothing to do with."

"What about Elmer?" asked Boots. "Those things are all his. He'll have a fit when he gets back."

"Either he gets upset or we all get expelled," said Bruno. "Take your choice."

"What are we going to do with it?" demanded Boots, beginning to panic.

"We can bury it," decided Bruno.

"That's ridiculous!" howled Boots. "Do you think The Fish won't notice a huge patch of turned-up earth?"

"The sand pit! We can bury it in the big sand pit by the road," insisted Bruno, "the one we use for high-jump."

"There's so much of it!" moaned Boots. "It would take us a month to bury all this!"

"That's why we have to have help," said Bruno. "We'll recruit some guys. Right now."

Both boys got up and headed for the door.

"I don't believe it!" muttered Bruno, looking back at the video machine. "I just don't believe it!"

*   *   *

Featherstone paced his small room, frowning. The latest fish broadcast had stated that the flying fish had flown away. That was no help—he knew it already. The flying fish was sitting on his night table. 'The pigs won't stay' obviously referred to the unfortunte incident with the pigpen and the farmer who hadn't believed him. There had been no reference to the meaning of the code letters M.H. The only new piece of information had been the introduction of the number 201. What it could mean, Featherstone had no idea.

His stomach rumbled and he remembered that he had missed dinner. The thought of another hamburger made him wince, and the diner across the road served nothing but sticky spaghetti, rubber sandwiches and concrete meat loaf. He had to have some variety. He picked up the telephone book and began to look in the Yellow Pages under 'Restaurants.'

An ad for a local eating place caught his eye. "Mister Halibut Fish and Chips," he read aloud. "201 Oak Road, Chutney." He closed the book. A strange feeling was coming over him, a feeling that there was something familiar about what he had just read. "201 Oak Road," he repeated, starting for the door.

He reached for the doorknob and froze. "201!" he exclaimed suddenly. "Mr. Halibut! *M.H.*! He opened the door and dashed down Main Street, still running as he turned onto Oak Road. There it was, Mister Halibut, with a large neon fish bordered by red and green chaser lights on the sign over the door. Red and green. The same code colours as on the M.H. Flying Fish! Yes, he could feel it. This unassuming place must be of great importance to the Fish's operation. And there was no mistake. The address was clearly marked as 201 Oak Road.

He opened the glass doors, walked in and stopped in his tracks. Seated at a corner table, his long nose buried in a basket of fish and chips, was the Fish himself—the man from room 14.

Featherstone's heart began to pound. He had finally done it, finally penetrated the Fish's iron curtain. Triumph over the Fish was very close now. He could smell victory!

His mind began to work furiously. He could not arrest the Fish now, where his agents would probably be close at hand. No, he must be a clever fisherman and lure the intended catch out to the local police station at the corner of Oak and Main.

Clasping his hands behind his back, Featherstone strolled among the tables, looking around nonchalantly and whistling. His eyes fell on the thin man and he feigned surprise.

"Oh, hi there," he said genially. "I've noticed we're staying at the same motel. Do you mind if I join you? My name's Featherstone."

The thin man was taken aback, but managed a friendly smile. "Certainly—sit down, sit down. My name is Hamilton."

Featherstone ordered his dinner and the two men chatted politely while eating.

At last Hamilton stirred his coffee and leaned back in his chair. "Well, I must say that was very good fish."

Featherstone was instantly alert. "Fish? Oh, yes, fish. Yes, very good indeed." His eyes narrowed. "I find myself very fond of fish lately."

"Me too," replied Hamilton. "Fishing is my hobby."

"Oh, fishing," said Featherstone. "Catching fish."

"Exactly," agreed Hamilton.

The waitress arrived with the two cheques.

"Well, I've certainly enjoyed having some company," said Featherstone heartily. "Why don't we walk along together?"

The two men paid their bills and strolled out onto the street, heading towards Main. As they neared the intersection, Featherstone pointed to the police station.

"Ah," he said, "a police station. I'll tell you what. As long as we're both stuck in this dull town, we ought to go in and study their street map. Maybe we can find something interesting."

Hamilton beamed radiantly. "That's a great idea!"

He's taking the bait, thought Featherstone as the two men stepped inside the building. This is it!

Once inside, both men suddenly wheeled to face each other and chorused, "I arrest you in the name of the law!"

There was a bewildered silence, then, "You can't arrest me!" cried Featherstone. "I'm arresting you! You're the Fish!"

"*I'm* the Fish? *You're* the Fish!" shouted Hamilton.

Featherstone whipped out his identification. "Sergeant Harold P. Featherstone, RCMP, Special Division."

Hamilton also produced a badge. "Leon Hamilton, Ontario Provincial Police."

"May I help you?" asked the desk sergeant.

"Stay out of this!" snapped Featherstone. "This is a police matter!" He turned to Hamilton. "You assaulted me in the dump!"

"I haven't been near the dump!" Hamilton protested. "You broke into my room!"

"I had a warrant!" shouted Featherstone. "You—you *are so* the Fish! I've got your code book to prove it!"

"Code book? That's not a code book, you jerk! I only bought it to try and identify the fish on TV!"

"You forced me off the road," accused Featherstone. "Right when the flying bomb was coming down!"

"I didn't force you off the road," yelled Hamilton. "You drove off. You stopped your car in the middle of the road and I almost hit you!"

"Well, what about the drive-in?" howled Featherstone.

"It was a lousy picture!"

"You stole my pop can when I went to the snack bar!" Featherstone insisted.

"No, I didn't!"

"But you were following me!"

"Well, of course I was following you!" bellowed Hamilton. "You're the Fish!"

"You tried to kill me! Twice!" accused Featherstone.

"The way you operate, you're lucky you don't kill yourself!" Hamilton scoffed.

"All right, you guys—" protested the desk sergeant.

"You lured me out on that lonely road and had a bomb launched at me!"

"I don't know any more about that bomb than you do!"

There was a moment of silence as the two men stared at each other in bewildered consternation. Featherstone, his face purple with rage, stood crouched, fists clenched. Hamilton towered over him, his knees bent, ready to spring. Finally Featherstone gingerly eased himself into a chair and held his head. His first big investigation lay in shambles. He had been so sure . . .

"You're not the Fish," he barely whispered.

"I've been telling you that," sighed Hamilton, his calm quickly returning. "I thought you were."

"Well," said Featherstone very quietly, "I'm not the Fish and you're not the Fish." He stood up and punched the wall. *"Then who the heck is?!"*

"Now, listen, you two," said the desk sergeant, "I don't know who you are or what you're talking about, but if you don't pipe down I'm going to throw you both in the cooler."

"We're police officers," said Hamilton, holding up his badge. Featherstone did likewise.

"So am I," sighed the desk sergeant. "Why don't you sit down and tell me all about it."

* * *

Shortly after midnight Bruno and Boots and six other boys began to carry all of Elmer's experiments and devices out of Dormitory 2 to be buried in the large sand pit by the road. Wilbur Hackenschleimer and Pete Anderson had the hole already dug when they got there.

"Dump everything in," ordered Bruno. "Boots, did you bring the salmon poster?"

"Yeah," Boots replied, "and the whole stack of them he had in his dresser."

"Good," said Bruno. "If The Fish ever sees that . . . "

Into the hastily dug hole went the video machine apparatus, some of which had had to be unbolted from the floor of room 201. Wires and cables followed. The entire contents of Elmer's chemistry lab, including remnants of his infamous cure for the common cold, went next. Bottles shattered and chemicals spilled out, mixing together and seeping into the sand. On top of that they dumped the remains of Operation Flying Fish—the remote control console and the launcher. Several assorted pieces of machinery, a few unidentified full beakers and test tubes, and the many salmon posters topped the tangled, smelly mess.

"That's everything," panted Larry Wilson.

"Good," sighed Bruno. "Let's cover it up."

Using shovels and hands, the boys heaped sand on top of Elmer's work.

"Poor Elmer," muttered Boots.

"At least he won't get expelled," Bruno pointed out. "And neither will we."

There was a muffled cry and the sand began shifting.

Larry looked around frantically. "Sidney! Sidney! We've buried *Sidney*!"

Madly the boys dug in and hauled Sidney Rampulsky out of the pit. Covered in sand, Sidney eyed the others reproachfully.

"You're not careful!" Larry raged. "You're just not careful!"

The boys heaped up the sand once again and headed quickly and quietly back to their rooms.

Take cover!

The next evening, in a corner of the squad room of the Chutney police station, Featherstone and Hamilton pored over a large map of Chutney and the surrounding district. They had been up all night comparing notes on their observations and experiences, and had been working most of the day on the map.

"Now," said Hamilton, "we've got a black X in every area where there've been complaints of fish broadcasts. Let's see if we can find out where they're coming from."

Both men studied the map intently for a moment.

"The area is round," commented Featherstone, to break the monotony.

"So it is," agreed Hamilton.

"As a matter of fact," added Featherstone, "it's almost a perfect circle. So—"

"So the broadcasts have to be coming from the centre of the circle," finished Hamilton. He laid a long, bony finger on the map. "That would be right here."

Featherstone beckoned to the desk sergeant and pointed to the centre of the circle. "What's located there?"

The man scratched his head. "Schools," he replied finally. "Yeah, two boarding schools, right across the road from each other."

"Schools," mused Hamilton. "That's impossible. Just children."

"Yes, definitely two schools," confirmed the sergeant. "One's a girls' finishing school called Scrimmage's, and the other's a boys' school. It's called Macdonald Hall."

"That's M.H.!" cried Featherstone. "*M.H. Flying Fish* was written on that bomb! This is what we've been looking for! Macdonald Hall!"

"But a bunch of kids?" protested Hamilton.

"Kids have teachers," Featherstone insisted in growing excitement, "and teachers are adults. One of those adults is the Fish!"

"The perfect cover," agreed Hamilton slowly. "No one would think to investigate for terrorist activity in a school. This Fish is a clever one."

"We don't know who we're after, so we'll have to restrict the whole place," decided Featherstone. "We'll need barriers and men. Sergeant, can you help us?"

"Well," offered the desk sergeant, "we've only got eight men on the Chutney force, but you can get any support you need from the county police."

"Good," said Featherstone. "Tonight we bring in the Fish!"

* * *

"What happened?" bawled Elmer Drimsdale, home from his field trip. "Where are all my things?" The room looked empty without all the equipment. The only things left were the plants and the ant colony. "What have you *done*?"

"We buried them," explained Bruno.

"You *what*?"

"Listen, Elmer, you're lucky we don't bury you too!" snapped Boots. "It's all your fault, you and your video machine!"

Elmer just stood there, stunned.

"You told us it would only broadcast to the screen on your black box!" accused Bruno. "That thing has been telecasting my fish jokes and your idiot salmon all over the county!"

"Remarkable!" breathed Elmer.

"Yeah, The Fish thought so too," said Bruno bitterly. "He was pretty sure it was us, but he couldn't prove it. So he called a big dorm inspection. We *had* to get rid of your stuff or the three of us would have been expelled!"

Elmer looked as if he were about to faint. "Expelled! I was almost expelled and I didn't even know it!" he exclaimed weakly. "You did the right thing! I hope you buried it deep enough!"

"Time will tell," said Boots. "And the next high jump."

"We passed inspection by the skin of our teeth," added Bruno. "We had to borrow a rug to cover up the holes in the floor where you bolted down the video machine."

"So we weren't caught, then?" asked Elmer in a small, hopeful voice.

"Hey," boasted Bruno, "I never get caught."

"Still," said Boots, "the way The Fish looked at us makes me nervous! He knows!"

"It was an honest mistake," babbled Elmer. "How was I to know that I would get such range without an antenna?"

"No one's blaming you, Elm," said Bruno kindly.

"I am," snapped Boots feelingly. "You get me into enough trouble. You don't need any help from Elmer."

"I'm a failure," lamented Elmer despondently. "I wanted so much to help save Macdonald Hall. I'm no good for anything."

"Don't be an idiot," said Bruno, glaring at Boots.

"That's just it," mourned Elmer. "I *am* an idiot."

Boots sighed. "You're a genius," he corrected firmly. "You've worked harder than anyone else on this project. It's just that—well, I guess even a genius fouls up once in a while."

"And you're our friend," said Bruno.

"And our roommate," added Boots.

Elmer brightened. "It's so good to have friends." He looked up at the bare wall where his beloved salmon poster had hung. "It's a good thing I have several more in the dresser.

Bruno looked at Boots. "No you don't," they chorused.

"We didn't get expelled," sighed Elmer, "but at what cost!"

* * *

Seven cars, their headlights out, pulled silently onto the soft shoulder of the highway near Macdonald Hall. Thirty shadowy figures left the cars and gathered in a group for a final briefing.

"Okay, men," said Featherstone, "this is it. I want the whole campus surrounded. Everyone is under restriction. No one goes in or out."

"What about the kids?" asked a Chutney patrolman.

"They don't go in or out either," said Hamilton. "Who knows how many the Fish has influenced."

"So watch them," cautioned Featherstone. "And remember, we don't want anyone hurt. When the Fish is cornered he may try to take the kids as hostages." He cleared his throat and raised his voice so the whole group could hear him. "We'll give you five minutes to spread out around the perimeter. Then Hamilton and I are going in with Kowalski and Baker."

The men stole away in the darkness to take up their assigned positions.

Featherstone, Hamilton and the two patrolmen got into Hamilton's unmarked car and turned into the Macdonald Hall driveway. Seeing a light on in the Faculty Building, they stopped the car in front of it and got out.

Mr. Sturgeon himself came out to greet him. "Good evening," he said courteously but without enthusiasm. "You gentlemen must be from the land developer's office. I've been told to expect you."

"Are you in charge here?" asked Featherstone.

"Yes, I'm the Headmaster. Sturgeon is my name."

"Sturgeon!" exclaimed Featherstone. "That's a kind of *fish*, isn't it?"

"How clever of you to have noticed," Mr. Sturgeon remarked, eyeing Featherstone coldly.

Whipping out his badge, Featherstone announced, "We've got you now, Fish!"

Mr. Sturgeon stared him him. "I beg your pardon?"

"Do you think we don't know what you've been doing? Did you think you could get away with it forever?" Featherstone was basking in the glory of his first capture. "Oh, no! We've got you now, Fish! You and your Fish Patrol are finished! The long arm of the law has caught up with you!" He nodded to the taller of the two patrolmen. "Take him, Kowalski."

Kowalski stepped forward and swiftly handcuffed himself to Mr. Sturgeon.

The Headmaster was livid. "What in the world do you think—"

Hamilton reached into the car and produced an electric megaphone. "*Attention!*" his voice boomed across the campus. "*Macdonald Hall is now under restriction! No one is to enter or leave the grounds! Repeat, no one is allowed to enter or leave!*"

"If you would kindly explain," Mr. Sturgeon insisted.

"You'll get all the explanation you want," snapped Featherstone, "in front of a judge!"

"But—"

The announcement had aroused the boys of Macdonald Hall and a swarm of them, headed by Bruno and Boots, stampeded onto the scene.

"Look!" blurted Bruno before he realized that he was shouting loud enough for the police and the Headmaster to hear. "Those guys have busted The Fish!"

Featherstone turned in horror to Hamilton. "Did you hear that? Even the kids know he's the Fish! There's nothing more contemptible than involving children in terrorist acts!" He faced Mr. Sturgeon. "I'm going to see that you're locked up for five hundred years!"

Mr. Sturgeon just stood there, shocked beyond words.

"What's going on?" asked one of the students.

"The Fish got busted!"

"But why?"

"I don't know!"

"They're taking him away!"

"I can't see anything!"

"Get off my foot!"

"What did The Fish do?"

"Probably robbed a bank!"

"I wonder how long he'll get?"

"Yep. That was it. He robbed a bank."

"This is all a ridiculous mistake!" insisted Mr. Sturgeon.

156

"Yeah, and you made it," jibed Hamilton with great satisfaction.

Near the entrance to the driveway the land developer's new black limousine pulled up and was stopped by three police officers. The developer rolled down his window.

"What's going on? I have a business appointment here."

"An appointment here, eh?" answered one of the officers. "Get out of the car, sir, and keep your hands where we can see them."

"What are you, nuts?"

"No, sir, not nuts," returned the policeman. "Just doing our job. Your chauffeur too, please. Both of you get into the first patrol car over there."

"Are we being arrested?" demanded the developer in bewilderment.

"No, sir, just detained. Into the patrol car, please. An officer will take your statement."

Hamilton's voice boomed across the campus again. *"Everybody keep calm! Everything is under control! There is no need for alarm!"*

The entire population of Macdonald Hall was milling around in confusion in front of the Faculty Building.

"Let him go!" bellowed Bruno at a nervous-looking Kowalski. "Whatever it is, he didn't do it! I can vouch for him!"

Mr. Sturgeon was still trying to reason with Featherstone. "Officer, if you will just listen to me!"

"You'll have plenty of time to talk," shouted Featherstone over the din, "when we get you and your Fish
Patrol down to the station."

"He's a nice guy!" shouted Bruno from the crowd.

"Yeah!" shouted many students in agreement.

Across the road Miss Scrimmage's P.A. system burst
into life with Cathy Burton's voice: *Attention, girls! Macdonald Hall is being invaded! They need our help! Let's
go!*

Instantly a stream of girls burst out through the door
and thundered across the highway to the Macdonald
Hall driveway. They did not even see the three officers
who made half-hearted attempts to block their way.
Scrimmage's girls were stopped by nothing. They
stampeded onto the campus and ran towards the crowd
of boys.

"Oh, no!" shouted Featherstone, appalled. "Is everyone in on this? Hamilton, do something!"

Girls were already mixing with the milling crowd of
boys, making the scene even more chaotic.

"*Go away!*" shouted Hamilton desperately over the
megaphone. "*Go back! This is a restricted area! Please go
away!*"

On her balcony Miss Scrimmage stood screaming at
her girls and waving her shotgun. "Girls! Girls, come
back here at once! Please come back!" She stubbed her
toe and tripped.

BOOM! The shotgun went off and pellets tore into the

sand of the high-jump pit just inside the Macdonald Hall grounds.

"It's that crazy lady!" shouted the developer in the shocked silence that followed the shotgun blast. "Arrest her! Don't let her near my new car!"

A loud, bubbling hiss rose from the pit as Elmer Drimsdale's spilled chemicals and equipment began to react to the disturbance beneath the thin layer of sand. Then the hiss faded and for a moment you could hear a pin drop.

Suddenly the silence was pierced by Elmer's half-crazed scream. *"Oh, no! Take cover!"*

At that very moment there was a tremendous explosion. The entire sand pit rose upward in a huge fireball, illuminating the dark campus. Sand, mingled with bits of the buried equipment, shot into the air. The crowd was engulfed in a rain of charred salmon posters. A second explosion followed, then a third, and finally what looked and sounded like a brilliant fireworks display.

"Hold your positions, men!" screamed Featherstone, crouching behind the flagpole as the barrage continued. A salmon poster fluttered down beside him and he stared at it in disbelief.

From her balcony Miss Scrimmage gazed in horror at the havoc below. "Help! Police!" she wailed.

"What's all this racket?" bellowed Coach Flynn from his window. The sight that met his eyes shocked him so much that he leaned over too far and toppled into the bushes around Dormitory 2.

"Everybody remain calm!" shrieked Hamilton's terrified voice over the megaphone. *"This is—"* the wind caught a salmon poster and slapped it right up against his face.

Abruptly the explosions ceased, and in the silence that followed, the howling of approaching sirens could be heard.

Timidly Bruno lifted his head in time to see a large fire engine roar up and stop beside the developer's blazing limousine. Miraculously, nothing else was on fire and no one seemed to be hurt.

"My car!" howled the developer from the floor of the police cruiser. His chauffeur was in tears. "That crazy woman blew up my new car!"

"Look!" exclaimed Boots breathlessly, pointing to the road. The highway was choked with cars, and a crowd of spectators stood on the edge of the campus staring curiously at the goings-on. Miss Scrimmage's lawn was completely covered by parked vehicles, among them the CHUT-TV mobile unit.

A man with a microphone bearing the call letters of a Toronto radio station was interviewing Sidney Rampulsky, who stood with a handkerchief to his bloody nose.

"No, I wasn't injured in the explosion," Sidney was saying. "I fell down."

News travels fast. More and more members of the media arrived on the scene in the hope of getting a good story out of what was going on at Macdonald Hall.

"It's an invasion," Cathy Burton was telling a crowd of reporters. She smiled for a photographer, her sweetest smile. "Right over there." She pointed to the flagpole where Mr. Sturgeon and the four policemen were just getting to their feet amid a confused crowd of students.

Not wanting to leave anyone out, Cathy turned to the crowd. "Right there! That's where the story is! By the flagpole! Over there!"

With Cathy in the lead, the entire swarm of reporters, interviewers, TV cameramen and photographers, as well as curious observers, converged on the flagpole.

Cathy snatched the confused Hamilton's megaphone and addressed the crowd. "*Here he is!*" she cried, indicating the dishevelled Mr. Sturgeon. "*He holds the answer to the whole thing! Take it away, sir!*"

Featherstone was sure he should have been doing something, but he could not imagine what. His training manual had let him down again.

Mr. Sturgeon was in the spotlight. All cameras were focused on him. Reporters stood there, pencils poised, waiting for his remarks.

Bruno Walton pushed his way through the crowd and ran to his Headmaster.

"I confess," he cried. "It's all my fault!"

Boots burst onto the scene and ran to his side. "And mine!"

Elmer Drimsdale appeared, stiff-lipped and straight-backed. "No!" he shouted dramatically. "I am responsible!"

Mr. Sturgeon gathered his dignity at last and rose to his full height, facing Kowalski.

"You will remove this ridiculous handcuff at once," he ordered quietly.

Kowalski looked at Featherstone who, hopelessly confused and uncertain, nodded feebly. The cuffs came off.

"You see," Bruno was explaining to the crowd of media people, "it all started when we found out that Macdonald Hall was going broke."

"Walton, that will do," said Mr. Sturgeon quietly.

Bruno turned an impassioned face to his Headmaster. "I don't think so, sir," he said earnestly. "Even though it's too late, I think everybody should know about Macdonald Hall." He turned back to the reporters amid a popping of flashbulbs. "About how a good school can go under in this day and age, and nobody knows or cares."

"*We care!*" chorused the student body of Macdonald Hall and Miss Scrimmage's combined.

"We sure do!" exlaimed Bruno. "And we've been trying to save our school." The orator in him fully aroused, Bruno was in high gear. "We tried to get publicity for our cause so that enrolment would go up and the school would be saved, but everything we did turned out wrong. We lost our pop cans, and none of Elmer's inventions worked properly, so we couldn't become famous, or set a world record, or be the home of some great invention and get great publicity that would save everything. It just didn't work out."

"What a human interest story!" exclaimed one of the reporters. "Go on! Go on!"

"Elmer was trying to invent a new kind of video," Bruno continued. "I didn't know it was broadcasting that fish to the whole county! I was just playing with it! And you were getting suspicous, sir. So to avoid any trouble we had to bury it—along with Elmer's other things, like his remote control device and his chemistry stuff. We buried all of it in the sand pit that used to be over there, and when Miss Scrimmage shot into it, I guess it blew up. And that's the whole story."

"We just couldn't let Macdonald Hall go down without a fight," added Boots.

They looked desperately at their Headmaster. He stood strangely still, saying nothing—

"So where do the police come in?" asked one of the reporters.

Featherstone snapped out of his trance. "Ah—yes," he began. "We were—uh—investigating. Isn't that right, Hamilton?"

"Yeah," said Hamilton. "That's it. Investigating."

"Oh, I get it," said the newsman. "You discovered Macdonald Hall's problem and you were helping them get publicity."

"Uh—right," said Featherstone gratefully.

"This is a very fine school," added Hamilton, "and it

shouldn't be allowed to close down. Today's police take an active interest in the education of our youth."

"Hey," said a photographer, "seeing as we missed the fireworks, let's get a shot of you two police guys shaking hands with the Headmaster."

Another photographer walked up to Bruno. "I'd like a shot of you and your two friends with the Headmaster."

"But why," asked someone, "did this Miss Scrimmage shoot bullets into the sand pit?"

"Oh, that was an accident," put in Cathy. "Miss Scrimmage never shoots anything on purpose."

Cameras clicked, pencils scribbled, video-tapes rolled. It was two hours before Mr. Sturgeon finally called a halt to the impromptu press conference, cleared the campus and sent his boys to bed.

Hot gazoobies!

"We're doomed!" muttered Boots mournfully as he, Bruno and Elmer walked across the campus towards the Faculty Building. Classes had been cancelled for the day because of the state of the campus, but Mr. Sturgeon had sent for the three boys right after lunch.

"I don't care," said Bruno. "Macdonald Hall is gone, but at least we sent it out in a blaze of glory." He reached down and picked up a partially burned salmon poster. "Here, Elmer."

"Thank you," said Elmer feebly, almost paralyzed with fear. "Do you think we'll be expelled?"

"You can't be expelled from a school that doesn't exist," observed Bruno gloomily. "We'll just go before everybody else, that's all."

"Still," sighed Boots, "my folks'll kill me!"

"If I had to be expelled," said Bruno, "this is the way I'd want it to happen—defending the Hall, whether The Fish appreciates it or not."

They entered the building and marched like martyrs to the Headmaster's office. Mr. Sturgeon himself ushered them inside and seated them, to their surprise, in the visitors' chairs rather than on the hard bench. They waited.

Mr. Sturgeon indicated a stack of newspapers on his desk. "You boys made quite an impression last night." He began to read headlines *"Loyal Students Fight to Save Financially Troubled School; Save Our School, Cry Macdonald Hall Boys; Fight to Save School Ends in Brilliant Explosion; Police Assist Battle to Keep School Solvent.* The list is endless. You were on network and local television last night and this morning, and on several radio stations. Two major magazines want to do articles on Macdonald Hall, and the *Science Gazette* would like to interview you, Drimsdale. Offhand I would say your efforts to get publicity were not entirely unsuccessful."

The three boys stared in silence.

"Listen to this editorial from the *Toronto Star*," the Headmaster went on. *"What kind of school spirit is it that inspired the boys of Macdonald Hall to try just about anything to save their school from bankruptcy? Only a rare institution and staff could bring out such loyalty and devotion. That is why today we take our hats off to the students of Macdonald Hall for their valiant and untiring efforts to keep their school operating...* The rest goes on to explain in detail the events of last night, with which I'm sure you are very familiar."

"Yes, sir," said Bruno meekly.

"I have some rather good news for all of us," Mr. Sturgeon went on. He permitted himself a small smile. "This morning alone we have had hundreds of telephone inquiries from parents all over the country. Already over forty new boys have been signed up for next year. We expect many more."

"Hot gazoobies!" blurted Bruno, jumping to his feet. He sat down quickly. "I mean—uh—that's very nice."

Mr. Sturgeon beamed. "Very nice indeed," he agreed. "We are planning to reopen Dormitory 3, and perhaps even build a Dormitory 4. I would like to congratulate you for your efforts."

"I'm not going to be expelled then, sir?" asked Elmer hopefully.

"Hardly," said Mr. Sturgeon. "I would venture a guess that you may even become famous. The *Science Gazette* is extremely interested in your video system and how you consistently overpowered the CHUT transmitter."

Elmer blushed. "It wasn't supposed to do that."

"And while we're on the subject, boys," said the Headmaster, "there are a few things I would really like clarification on." He cleared his throat carefully. "Recently I have received a series of complaints and accusations from Miss Scrimmage concerning various—uh—alleged activities. For instance, does anyone know if Miss Scrimmage was actually, as she phrased it, 'beaten up'?"

"That would have to be when Sidney Rampulsky fell

on her," offered Bruno thoughtfully.

"Of course it was an accident, sir," added Boots quickly.

Mr. Sturgeon nodded slowly. "With him it always is. And I suppose you have an explanation for a phantom shoe that Miss Scrimmage found after an alleged raid?"

Boots hung his head. "Yes, sir. That was mine."

"I see," said the Headmaster. "What about Miss Scrimmage's story of a member of the Macdonald Hall staff running around her school in his underclothes?"

"Oh, that was just Coach Flynn, sir," said Bruno. "But it was his gym shorts, not his underwear. He doesn't know anything about it, though. He was drunk at the time."

"I beg your pardon?" snapped Mr. Sturgeon stiffly.

"You see," explained Boots, "we put Elmer's cold cure in his Muscle-Ade and he drank it, and it made him— well . . . "

"Intoxicated," supplied Elmer. "My cold remedy reacts badly to the citric acid in those high-energy drinks."

"So when the coach drank it," added Bruno, "he got sort of drunk and went over to Scrimmage's and carried on. But it wasn't his fault."

"He didn't even know about it."

"Perhaps it's just as well," said Mr. Sturgeon with a queer smile.

"Is there anything else you'd like to know about, sir?" asked Bruno.

168

"Just one more thing comes to mind," said the Headmaster. "Would there be anything in Drimsdale's equipment that Miss Scrimmage might misconstrue as a red and green flying bomb?"

Elmer choked and had to be pounded heartily on the back by his two roommates.

"It was the M.H. Flying—uh—remote control device, sir," stammered Bruno.

"Ah, yes," said Mr. Sturgeon. "That would be the flying *fish*, the one that flew away."

"Yes, sir."

"That will be all," said Mr. Sturgeon. "You are dismissed. However, may I suggest that the next time you embark on a crusade such as this you inform me and obtain permission for your activities. Good day."

* * *

The entire population of Macdonald Hall was assembled on the front lawn by the highway.

"Okay!" shouted Bruno. "The girls have to hear us, so be sure and yell loud! All together, now—one, two, three . . ."

A great chant rose from their throats, "*Macdonald Hall is saved! Macdonald Hall is saved!*"

A stream of girls erupted from Miss Scrimmage's Finishing School for Young Ladies. Led by Cathy Burton and chased by their teachers, they stampeded across the lawn, lined up across the road from the boys and joined in the chant.

"*MACDONALD HALL IS SAVED! MACDONALD HALL IS SAVED!*"

* * *

Saturday dawned warm and sunny, and Macdonald Hall's boys were all sleeping in. Friday night there had been a big victory party that had lasted far into the night and the students were exhausted from their celebrating.

A large poster bearing the message *We Saved Macdonald Hall* was draped across Bruno Walton's head as the three inhabitants of room 201 began to stir.

"It's the middle of the night," yawned Bruno.

"No," said Boots. "Actually, there's a poster covering your face."

"Oooh," moaned Elmer. "I have a headache!"

"That was a decent party," said Bruno, peeling the poster off and dropping it onto the floor. "Too bad the girls couldn't be there. That Miss Scrimmage sure carries a grudge. Just because the police confiscated her shotgun, she's mad at us."

Boots eased himself out of bed and walked over to the window for a breath of air. He looked, then stared, outside. "Bruno—Bruno, I think you'd better see this."

"See what?" asked Bruno groggily.

"Come and see," Boots insisted.

Bruno staggered over to the window, looked out and

let out a bellow of rage. There, prominent on Miss Scrimmage's front lawn, gleamed the world's largest tin-can pyramid, more than sixteen feet tall. Parked in front of the wrought-iron gates of the school was the CHUT-TV mobile unit, and directly behind it a large, bright blue van bearing the words *Rankin Book of World Records.*

"*My* pyramid!" shrieked Bruno in hysterics. "She stole *my* pyramid! I'll *kill* her!" Before Boots could stop him, he had scrambled out the window and was running across the campus in his pyjamas.

Boots leaped out and ran barefoot across the grass in hot pursuit. Elmer, confused and astonished, followed.

Bruno ran to the edge of the highway, but was prevented from crossing by Boots and Elmer, who flanked him, each holding onto an arm for dear life.

"Cathy! Cathy! That's *my* pyramid! *Mine*! You'll *pay* for this!"

Cathy waved in a friendly manner, but said nothing.

"I'll call the police!" Bruno threatened darkly. "I'll call the army! I'll call *Mr. Sturgeon*!"

Boots and Elmer began hauling him back towards Dormitory 2.

"I'll have your *head* for this!" shouted Bruno, his heels dragging. "I'll file a complaint! I'll write my Member of Parliament! . . . the Prime Minister! . . . the Queen! . . . "

Cathy watched as Boots and Elmer hauled him out of sight, until his voice was just a faint echo. "He seems upset about something," she commented mildly.

Featherstone out

REPORT TO:	RCMP, Special Division, Ottawa.
SUBJECT:	Interference with TV broadcasting in Chutney, Ontario, and surrounding area.
OFFICER ASSIGNED:	Sgt. Harold P. Featherstone, Jr.

I began my investigation by observing several interfering broadcasts, all calling attention to an individual known as the Fish. Despite a Headquarters briefing indicating the possible development of terrorist activity, I instantly deduced that the broadcasts were the work of amateurs. Through careful investigation, I managed to connect these broadcasts with several unusual incidents occurring in the Chutney area. Information resulting from my investigations led me to Macdonald Hall, a boys' school located south of Chutney. At that time I made sparing use of the local police force, and received minor assistance from an OPP officer.

I discovered, as I had suspected throughout, that the broadcasts were being made unwittingly by a group of students at Macdonald Hall, who referred to their Headmaster as "The Fish," his name being Sturgeon. Since their school was in financial trouble, they were seeking publicity. I, of course, used my influence to see that they received it. All involved were very grateful to me and to Special Division, since the school's financial problems have now been resolved.

SPECIAL EXPENSES:

Repairs to automobile	$1129.61
Reimbursement to farmer for damage to pigpen	95.00
1 pair shoes	49.95
1 window screen, room 14, Chutney Motel	19.00
1 book, *Fish of the World*	2.99
1 can deodorant	1.79 tax incl.
TOTAL	$1298.34

Sergeant Harold P. Featherstone, Jr.

About the Author

Gordon Korman wrote his first book, *This Can't Be Happening at Macdonald Hall*, as a seventh grade English project. By the time Korman had graduated from high school he had written and published five other books including *Go Jump in the Pool!*, *Beware the Fish!*, and *The War with Mr. Wizzle* all available in Apple Paperback editions from Scholastic Inc. Korman in now studying film and screenwriting at New York University. Between semesters he finds time to answer piles of fan mail and make personal appearances across the country.